ERIC J. POLLI

10th Round

TRUE
GRIT
PUBLISHING

First published by True Grit 2025

Copyright © 2025 by Eric J. Polli

All rights reserved. No part of this publication may be reproduced, stored or transmitted in any form or by any means, electronic, mechanical, photocopying, recording, scanning, or otherwise without written permission from the publisher. It is illegal to copy this book, post it to a website, or distribute it by any other means without permission.

This novel is entirely a work of fiction. The names, characters and incidents portrayed in it are the work of the author's imagination. Any resemblance to actual persons, living or dead, events or localities is entirely coincidental.

Eric J. Polli asserts the moral right to be identified as the author of this work.

Designations used by companies to distinguish their products are often claimed as trademarks. All brand names and product names used in this book and on its cover are trade names, service marks, trademarks and registered trademarks of their respective owners. The publishers and the book are not associated with any product or vendor mentioned in this book. None of the companies referenced within the book have endorsed the book.

First edition

ISBN: 9798218831998

Proofreading by Kelly Messier

This book was professionally typeset on Reedsy.
Find out more at reedsy.com

..For my Aunt Tina —
my beloved TT.
You lifted everyone around you with quiet strength and endless love.
You never sought the spotlight, yet your light reached everyone who knew you.
Your laughter, your grace, your heart — they live on in every moment of peace and
kindness I find.
This book is for you, and because of you.

Did you ever know that you're my hero?
And everything I would like to be?
I can fly higher than an eagle,
For you are the wind beneath my wings

Contents

Foreword   iii

Preface   iv

Prologue   1

I   10th Round

 1   Out from the Shadows   7

 2   Not Dead Yet   14

 3   Voices from the Past   19

 4   The Son   28

 5   Young Fire   35

 6   Bottom of the Canvas   40

 7   It Starts Now   45

 8   I'd Really Love to See You Tonight   52

 9   My Girl   59

10   History at the Door   63

11   Secrets   69

12   In Case You Never Hear It   73

13   Love Hurts   78

14   Moment of Truth   83

15   Flashbulbs and Shadows   87

16   Junkyard Dogs   91

17   Help Me   96

18   The Empty Ring   102

19   Fight Night   108

20   The Walk Back   114

21 One Final Fight   118
22 Last Round   123

Foreword

When I first read 10th Round, what hit me wasn't just the boxing—it was the truth in it. The way the story captures what it feels like to be a fighter, to keep getting back up when life keeps knocking you down. That's not something you can fake. You either lived it or you didn't. And I could tell right away that whoever wrote this understands what that life is really about.

Boxing's not just about throwing punches. It's about pain, sacrifice, and heart. It's about the people who stand in your corner when no one else will. This book gets that. It reminded me of the quiet moments after a fight— when the crowd's gone, your body's beat up, and you start thinking about everything you gave up chasing a dream.

Mickey Brannigan—the main character—felt real to me. I've known guys like him. Hell, I've been that guy at times—a fighter trying to hold on, trying to make peace with the past while still teaching the next generation what it means to have heart. That's what 10th Round is really about. It's not just boxing. It's about life, redemption, and finding a reason to keep fighting.

I think anyone who's ever been through something tough—inside the ring or outside of it—will feel this story. It's honest, it's emotional, and it's got that grit that makes you remember why we fight in the first place.

I'm proud to write this foreword because 10th Round isn't just a boxing story. It's a story about being human

— *"Irish" Micky Ward*
former World Champion from Lowell Massachusetts

Preface

I grew up in a suburban town north of Boston called North Andover. I was fortunate to be raised in a home with two solid parents—both self-employed, both self-made, both determined to build a better life for their family. They started their own businesses straight out of high school and worked tirelessly to make sure my sister and I never went without. From them, I learned what it meant to work hard, stay motivated, and do everything in life with passion and enthusiasm.

I was also blessed with great grandparents and a wonderful sister who I was eight years older than. As a kid, I was a mix of extrovert and introvert—someone who loved meaningful conversation but also craved solitude. My quiet moments were when my imagination thrived. Even in middle school, I would find myself daydreaming during class, coming up with stories for movies, books, or TV shows. I didn't know it then, but those wandering thoughts were the earliest signs of a creative restlessness that would stay with me forever.

In high school, I was drawn to stories—to English classes where characters felt real and words carried weight. I graduated from St. John's Prep in 2005, and I still remember sitting in Mr. David Edson's class, reading novels that challenged how I saw the world. I wasn't much for math or science, but storytelling spoke to me. It always did.

Outside the classroom, my imagination lived on movie screens and wrestling arenas. I'd watch The Shawshank Redemption, The Godfather, Goodfellas, Scarface, and every Rocky movie more times than I can count. The Rocky series, especially, became a kind of emotional language for me—a story about resilience, redemption, and the will to keep fighting. As a kid, I was also a huge fan of professional wrestling. I knew it wasn't real, but the storylines fascinated me—the entrances, the music, the emotions. I wasn't hooked on the matches; I was hooked on the storytelling.

Boxing fascinated me too. My neighbor and I would spend afternoons pretending to be Rocky and Apollo, trading punches with oversized gloves and bigger dreams. Those moments weren't just play—they were early glimpses of the kind of stories I'd someday want to tell: stories about flawed men fighting to find themselves again.

After graduating from Merrimack College with a degree in political science, I thought I'd enter the world of politics. I struggled to find work, though, and ended up coaching youth basketball on the side. That side job slowly turned into a career—one I built from the ground up, just like my parents did. I founded a company called Mass Elite Basketball in 2008, and eventually, it grew into something larger: a program that impacted hundreds of young athletes and families.

But like many things I pour myself into, it consumed me. I gave it everything—my time, my energy, my weekends, my focus—often at the expense of moments with the people I loved. I missed birthdays, family dinners, and holidays because of the game of basketball. It gave my life structure and purpose, but it also demanded a cost I didn't fully understand at the time.

In May 2024, two things happened that changed me forever. First, I became an uncle. My niece didn't like me much at first—I was too loud, too big of a personality—but that changed quickly. Holding her gave me something I hadn't felt in years: perspective. Around that same time, I was also let go from the organization that had purchased my company, Mass Elite. Losing something I had built from scratch was painful—but in hindsight, it was one of the best things that ever happened to me.

Those two moments—the birth of my niece and the loss of my business— gave me clarity. They reminded me that time is the most precious thing we have, more valuable than money or material success. For the first time in years, I had time to breathe, to think, and to create.

That's when I started writing again.

Writing gave me a sense of peace I hadn't felt in a long time. It was therapeutic. I wanted to create a character who was neither good nor evil—someone who lived in the gray areas, just like most of us do. That's how Mickey Brannigan was born. Mickey is a man who climbed to the top of the boxing world but lost almost everything that mattered along the way. He chased things that could never love him back and neglected the people who truly did. He's deeply flawed, but in his final days, he's searching for forgiveness and redemption—not from the world, but from himself.

When I wrote 10th Round, I wanted it to be a story about hope, love, and regret. It's about a man realizing too late that the things he spent his life chasing were never what truly mattered. It's about the relationships we break and the ones we fight to mend before the clock runs out.

For me, writing this book was more than a creative project—it was a reminder that time is fleeting, that redemption is real, and that even in our lowest moments, we still have the power to make things right.

This book is for anyone who's ever lost something, rebuilt themselves, or searched for forgiveness in places they once took for granted. It's for those who have fallen, failed, and fought their way back. It's for the dreamers, the doubters, and the ones still swinging when life feels like it's in the final round.

— *Eric J. Polli*

Prologue

Topsfield, Massachusetts — October 1988

The air smelled like kettle corn, hay, and wood smoke—that unmistakable New England mix that only came once a year. The Topsfield Fair stretched across the fairgrounds like something out of a postcard.

Mickey Brannigan walked through the crowd with his wife, Maria, and their little boy, Danny, who was balanced on his hip. People turned as he passed—a few clapped him on the back, others called out his name.

"Champ!" someone shouted from behind a row of food stands. "Mickey Brannigan, the pride of Massachusetts!"

He grinned and gave a wave, his other arm tightening around Danny. "You hear that, kid?" he said. "Your old man's a big deal."

Danny giggled and reached out toward a helium balloon drifting overhead. Maria smiled—that easy, proud smile that made Mickey feel like the luckiest man alive. Her scarf blew across her face as the wind picked up, and she brushed it away, tucking her arm through his.

It had been nearly two years since Mickey had become the Middleweight Champion of the World. His picture had been in Sports Illustrated, his face on TV. Endorsement deals were coming in faster than he could answer the phone. But here, at the Topsfield Fair, surrounded by families and laughter and falling leaves, the noise of the world felt far away.

A young man in a Red Sox cap asked for an autograph. Mickey signed the napkin, still holding Danny in his arm. Another fan shook his hand and told him he'd stayed up late to listen to the fight on the radio. Maria watched, smiling as Mickey bent down to talk to a little boy holding a toy boxing glove.

"Keep your hands up, champ," Mickey said to the kid, giving him a wink.

"And always listen to your mother."

As they moved on, Maria leaned in close. "You love this, don't you?"

"What's not to love?" Mickey said. "I got the belt, I got my family, I got my health. Everything I'll ever need."

Maria squeezed his arm, and for a moment, Mickey felt like the whole world had lined up just right. The smell of apple cider and fried dough hung in the air, kids were laughing somewhere near the petting zoo, and the leaves were turning that deep, perfect shade of red you only get in New England for a couple of weeks each year.

They stayed until the fair began to close, the lights dimming, the crowd thinning out. Mickey carried Danny on his shoulders as they walked to the car, Maria's hand resting lightly on his back.

When they pulled into the driveway of their home in Boxford, the house looked almost unreal in the stillness—white clapboard, black shutters, a yard that rolled out like a golden ocean of fallen leaves. Maria took Danny inside, humming softly as she went upstairs. Mickey lingered in the doorway for a moment, then stepped out into the yard.

The crickets had started up, the air smelled faintly of pine, and the sun was just disappearing behind the trees. He slipped his hands into his jacket pockets and looked out over the lawn. The championship belt was sitting on the kitchen counter inside, glinting beneath the soft light.

He thought about all the years it had taken—the bruises, the cuts, the nights in cheap hotels, the people who said he'd never make it. And now, here he was. The house, the wife, the son, the title. Everything a man could ever want.

For the first time in a long time, Mickey felt completely still inside.

"I got everything," he whispered to himself. "Everything I'll ever need."

The last of the sunlight flickered across the trees, and for one fleeting moment, it felt like time itself had stopped—like the whole world was holding its breath, content to let him believe it could stay that way forever.

But time doesn't stop, not even for champions. And years later, when the cheers had faded and the lights had gone out, Mickey Brannigan would look back on that autumn evening and realize it was the last time life ever felt perfect.

I

10th Round

This book isn't just a boxing story.
It's also a story of endings. The last round of a life. The moment
when the bell is about to ring for the final time and you're faced
with the only questions that matter: How do you want to finish
your story? What kind of legacy do you want to leave behind?
This book is for anyone who has ever been knocked down. For
anyone who has felt the weight of regret or the ache of unfinished
business. For anyone who has ever wondered if they could get back
up.

1

Out from the Shadows

Dawn crept over the streets of South Boston, casting a pale light on the cracked pavement of West Broadway. A weathered black sedan rolled quietly along the curb, its paint chipped and rust nibbling away at the wheel wells. A faded Red Sox bumper sticker clung to the back like a forgotten piece of pride.

Inside, Mickey Brannigan sat behind the wheel, his face carved by years of punches and pain. Sixty-three years old, with the hardened eyes of a man who'd spent a lifetime trading blows—in and out of the ring. On the dash, dangling from a frayed piece of string, hung an old rabbit foot he'd kept since his fighting days. It was his father's.

On the passenger seat sat a worn, stained gym bag. Everything about Mickey was tired but taut—like a boxer at the end of the final round, still standing but swaying.

He passed O'Connor's Tavern—or what used to be O'Connor's. The sign was gone now, the brick façade boarded up and tagged with spray paint. It used to be a place where fighters crowded around a broken TV to watch the Friday Night Fights. Mickey slowed for half a block, staring at the boarded windows. For a second, he swore he could still hear the cheers inside—then the empty street swallowed the sound. He pressed the gas.

Mickey wasn't admiring the city. He scanned the streets like a man searching for ghosts—remnants of who he once was, who he could have been.

The streets looked the same, but the faces had changed. New storefronts and different graffiti. It made him feel both invisible and obsolete.

He pulled up to a building. "Chopper's Gym," the rusted sign read. The paint peeled like old tape, but the place still stood. Barely.

Mickey parked. He didn't move for a moment. Just stared at the entrance as it might swallow him whole. His fingers tapped lightly on the steering wheel, a nervous rhythm born of decades in the ring.

Then, he reached into his jacket pocket and pulled out a small pill bottle.

The label spelled it out in quiet certainty. He stared at it, his thumb brushing the plastic. Then, with a sigh that seemed to deflate his entire chest, he tossed it into the glove box and stepped out of the car.

His boots hit the pavement. Solid. Heavy. Familiar.

The front door creaked open. Inside, the gym smelled like dust and sweat. Heavy bags swayed faintly in still air. On the wall, a poster of Mickey in his prime—gloves raised, chest out, championship belt gleaming—hung crooked, faded but proud. It had yellowed around the edges, but the fire in his eyes still burned.

Coach "Chopper" McNeil stood inside the ring, barking instructions to a wiry young fighter as he worked the pads. His voice hadn't changed—a raspy bark that could cut through music and muscle alike. He didn't see Mickey at first. But then the door creaked again.

Chopper turned slowly. His grizzled face locked eyes with Mickey's. Silence.

"You're either a ghost… or you're finally dying," Chopper said.

Mickey cracked a faint smile. "Maybe both."

Mickey leaned against the ropes while Chopper stood nearby with a towel slung over one shoulder.

Chopper didn't look amused. "You look like hell," he muttered.

"That bad?" Mickey replied with a chuckle.

"You disappear for over a decade," Chopper said, "and now you show up looking like a bag of laundry somebody found in an alley."

Mickey didn't answer right away. He looked around the gym, taking it all in like an old photograph. The same smell, same creaks in the floorboards.

It was the only place that ever made him feel whole—and the place he'd abandoned when things fell apart.

The two men stared at each other. Years hung between them, thick with regret and pride.

* * *

It was the summer of 1976, the heat in South Boston thick as soup, and Mickey Brannigan was nineteen years old with blood on his knuckles and nowhere to be. His old man had died that spring—massive heart attack in the middle of the night. Just like that, the only anchor he ever had was gone. No warning. No goodbye.

Mickey hadn't cried at the funeral. Not because he didn't want to—he just didn't know how. His father was a hard man, but a steady one. And when he went, so did the last bit of structure in Mickey's life. He dropped out of community college two weeks later. Got fired from the dock for punching a foreman who called him "useless." And then he just started fighting. Bars, alleys, street corners. Anyone looked at him wrong, said something sideways—he was swinging.

Not for glory. Not for pride. He was trying to feel something. Anything.

That was how he ended up outside a dive on Dorchester Avenue one night, blood on his shirt, split lip, and a gash above his right eye. The guy he fought was bigger, drunker, and definitely had friends. Mickey was sitting on the curb, holding his ribs and wondering if this was it—if he was just going to be another neighborhood burnout.

That's when the old man showed up.

"Hell of a left hook," the voice said.

Mickey looked up. The guy had silver hair slicked back, a cigar in his mouth, he'd seen every bad decision a man could make and survived them all. He was wearing a leather jacket in 90-degree heat.

"You a scout or something?" Mickey asked.

"No. I'm a trainer," the man said. "Name's Chopper McNeil. Used to work with pros—real ones. But I like rebuilding wreckage better."

Mickey laughed bitterly, wincing at the pain in his side from the fight.

"You come by Southie Boxing Club tomorrow morning. Seven sharp. Don't be late. I don't wait on punks."

He walked off, just like that. Left Mickey bleeding on the curb.

The next morning, Mickey didn't go. But the day after that, he did. He walked into Southie Boxing Club with a swollen eye and an attitude. The gym smelled like sweat.

Chopper was there already, barking orders at some kid hitting the heavy bag. Mickey stood in the doorway.

Chopper didn't look up. "You're two days late."

That was the beginning. Chopper didn't coddle him. Didn't ask about his father. Didn't ask about the fights. He just trained him. Hard. Brutal. Old-school. Made him run in boots. Spar with pros. Taught him how to take a hit and keep moving.

"You're not a street fighter anymore," Chopper would growl. "You're a boxer."

Over time, the rage started to have direction. The pain started to mean something. And slowly, Mickey stopped being lost. He never said it out loud, but Chopper saved his life. Not by hugging him or ever saying that he loved him, but by giving him something to fight for.

Now decades later, Chopper grabbed a stool and sat down.

Chopper's stare hardened. "I haven't seen you in over eight years. Why are you here?"

"I don't know," Mickey admitted. "I just needed somebody... familiar."

Chopper studied him. His voice dropped. "You sick or something?"

Mickey didn't answer. He only gave a slight nod, shoulders heavy with the weight of truth. Chopper's lips tightened.

"Christ almighty," Chopper whispered.

"Six months," Mickey said finally, voice low. "Maybe less. Doc said I could try treatment, but what will that really do?"

"You always were too damn stubborn to listen to anybody," Chopper growled.

"If it's my time, Chop... then it's my time."

"And Danny?" Chopper asked quietly.

Mickey looked away. "He doesn't know."

"Well, he needs to find out."

"I know."

Silence stretched between them. Chopper leaned forward, elbows on his knees, his eyes not leaving.

"You remember the first week you walked in here?" he asked. "Full of piss and vinegar. Wouldn't shut up about how you didn't need nobody."

Mickey almost smiled. "And you made me run five miles in steel-toed boots. My toenails almost fell off. Thought you were trying to kill me."

"Maybe I was. Just a little." Chopper smirked. "But you finished it, didn't you?"

"Didn't have a choice."

"Damn right. I told you back then—you start something, you finish it."

Mickey's eyes fell to the floor. "Guess I never finished much, did I?"

"Don't start that poor-me shit," Chopper snapped. "I ain't in the mood for pity or stupidity."

"It's the truth," Mickey said, voice cracking under the weight. "I lost the belt. I gave up Maria. I lost my son. Fuck—I didn't even go to Ma's funeral."

Chopper's jaw tightened. "You can still fix some of that, Mick. Danny's still here."

"He wants nothing to do with me."

"I still remember him," Chopper said softly. "Sitting on the ring step when he was what—six? Seven? Watching every punch you threw. Didn't matter if you were sparring a tomato can or a world beater. He thought you were Superman."

Mickey swallowed hard. "And I went and showed him Clark Kent was just some drunk with bad knees."

"No," Chopper said firmly. "You showed him you were human. He didn't need perfect, Mick. He just needed his old man."

The silence that followed was heavy, thick with things left unsaid. Mickey rubbed his hands together, the sound dry and nervous. Chopper's eyes never left him.

"There's a cot in the back," Chopper said finally. "Smells like mold, so you'll feel right at home."

Mickey smirked, the first real smile he'd managed since walking in.

"And Mick…" Chopper added, his tone turning rough again. "Don't die in my goddamn gym."

Mickey didn't answer aloud. He just nodded, slowly. The truth hung in the air like smoke.

Mickey had never been much for family. Not because he didn't want one, but because life had a way of giving him the wrong kind of examples. His old man had been a shadow—the kind you could never quite catch, always disappearing when you needed him most.

Chopper McNeil filled that gap without even meaning to. He wasn't gentle, and he sure as hell wasn't the kind of man to put a hand on your shoulder and say he was proud. Chopper's version of encouragement was telling you that you looked like hell and then making you run five extra miles.

He called you "kid" long after you were a grown man. He barked at you when you were late, and if you ever complained, he'd give you a look that could knock the wind out of you faster than any punch.

But under all that, Mickey knew. He knew in the way Chopper showed up when no one else did—the way he'd bail him out of a bad situation, stand in his corner when the whole world was against him, and never once walk away when things got ugly.

Chopper didn't need to say he loved him. Men like that didn't talk about love. They lived it, in their own rough-edged way.

And somewhere along the line, Mickey realized that when he thought about the man who taught him how to fight, how to stand his ground, and how to take the hits life threw at him, he wasn't thinking about his father. He was thinking about Chopper.

The first night Mickey ever stayed overnight in the gym, he didn't know if he'd make it till morning. Not because it was unsafe—hell, Chopper's gym was the safest he'd ever felt—but because the silence was different there. It wasn't the kind of silence that pressed in on you. It was the kind that gave you room to breathe.

He remembered the smell of canvas and liniment, the faint hum of the soda machine in the corner, and the way the ring sat under the dim lights.

He'd thrown his bag down in the little back room—just a cot, a dresser with one drawer that worked, and a bare bulb hanging from the ceiling. No TV. No radio. No distractions.

There was something about it. The steady drip of the leaky sink in the bathroom. The faint thud of a heavy bag still swinging from earlier in the day. The echoes of the day's sparring matches lingering in the walls.

And maybe that's why it felt like home—because there was no pretending in a place like that. No polished furniture to impress guests, no lawn to mow for appearances. Just sweat, work, and the smell of leather.

His body was giving out on him now. The doctors had been clear. He wasn't coming back from this fight. Every step felt heavier, as if he was carrying the weight of all the rounds he'd ever fought.

But when he pushed open that old door and saw the cot in the corner, he felt the same strange comfort he had all those years ago.

He sat on the edge of the bed, letting his hand rest on the worn frame. The room was still quiet, still simple. No photographs on the wall, no trophies lined up on a shelf. Just space to think. Space to be.

The silence wasn't empty—it was familiar. Almost kind. It wrapped around him like old gloves, beaten soft over time.

In the eighties and nineties, he'd gone home to places with bigger rooms, softer beds, and fine curtains that blocked out the morning sun. But they'd never felt like this.

This room didn't ask anything of him. It didn't care whether he was champion or washed-up, healthy or dying.

And for the first time in weeks, Mickey let himself lean back on the thin mattress, close his eyes, and stop fighting.

A new day had started.

Mickey Brannigan had returned.

2

Not Dead Yet

When Mickey opened his eyes again, the room was darker—only a thin slice of light cutting through the crack in the door. The smell of old leather and sweat still hung in the air, faint but familiar. For a second, he wasn't sure what had woken him. Then he heard it.

Thump.

The sound of gloves snapping against the heavy bag. Not wild swings, but measured, disciplined shots. A rhythm.

He swung his legs over the side of the cot, the floor cool under his bare feet. His joints ached like rusted hinges, but he didn't rush. He just sat there for a moment, letting the sound guide him.

It wasn't Chopper in there. Wasn't any of the old crew. It was a young man by the name of Tyrell Banks.

Mickey stood, gripping the door-frame for balance before making his way down the hall. His knuckles brushed the peeling paint as he walked, and the faint buzz of a fluorescent bulb above filled the silence between punches. He stopped just outside the main floor, leaning against the wall so the kid wouldn't notice him right away.

Tyrell was working the bag as if it owed him money. Sweat dripped from his chin, his eyes locked dead ahead. There was no wasted motion, no showboating. Just the kind of focus Mickey remembered having himself when he was young and hungry.

Mickey leaned in the doorway, watching. The kid's form was raw, but there was something there—that same wild spark Chopper had once accused Mickey of wasting.

The kid was a storm in sneakers. He moved as if he had something to prove.

Mickey saw someone with a lot of tools, but he also saw his weaknesses. Chopper always told him that "even the best fighters need to be taught the little things." The things that not just win you fights, but win you world titles.

Mickey leaned against the wall, coffee steaming in his hand, the rising curl of it blurring his tired vision, watching.

"Rope's got better footwork than you," he said, voice low and sandpapered.

Tyrell paused mid-skip. "What?"

"You're skipping like you're scared of the floor."

A smirk tugged at Tyrell's mouth—the kind young men wear like armor. "You the new janitor?"

Mickey ignored the jab. "You always up this early?"

"Mind don't shut off," Tyrell said.

Mickey nodded. He understood that kind of mind—the kind that kept you moving long after the world thought you were finished.

Tyrell followed Mickey's gaze toward the small office at the back of the gym, where old fight posters lined the wall like fading prayers.

"That you up there?"

"Maybe," Mickey said.

"Brannigan, right? Middleweight champ from the stone age?"

"Stone age treated me alright."

Tyrell grinned. "Heard you had a chin. Zero defense."

"I preferred punching to thinking."

"Looks like it caught up."

Mickey took the hit with a small smile. He'd been hit worse.

Tyrell returned to the rope—faster now, part challenge, part performance. Mickey watched the kid's feet, not the showmanship. The rhythm was off. Beautiful in its way, but off.

"Name?" Mickey asked.

"Tyrell Banks," he said. "Golden Gloves. Turning pro soon. Chopper says

I'm the real deal."

"They say that to everybody."

"Yeah," Tyrell said, "but I don't get hit."

Mickey let out a breath that wasn't quite a laugh.

"You will."

Tyrell dropped the rope and stepped closer, chin up with youthful certainty.

"No offense—different era. Guys like me don't need old-school bruisers teaching us."

"Maybe I don't need to waste words on somebody who hasn't bled yet."

Tyrell opened his mouth with another comeback ready, then thought better of it, settling for a smirk.

Mickey rose slowly from the stool. He stepped in close enough that Tyrell could smell the stale coffee and winter air on him.

"It ain't speed," Mickey said.

"It's rhythm. Change rhythm, you change the fight."

Tyrell didn't want to listen, but he did.

The truth had a way of slipping through, no matter how thick the pride.

"Nah," Tyrell said at last, "I'm all set with the lessons."

"Everybody is," Mickey replied. "Right up until they're staring at the ceiling."

For the first time, Tyrell hesitated. Just enough for Mickey to see the crack.

Tyrell turned away and attacked the heavy bag—crisp, sharp punches, all precision and no history. Mickey narrowed his eyes, studying the legs, the hips, the balance.

The kid was good. But he had never been hit by the world yet, only by bags that didn't swing back.

From the doorway, Chopper appeared, sipping his morning bitterness from an old coffee mug.

"You sizing him up," Chopper said, "or just killing time?"

"Kid's got confidence."

"Confidence is cheap," Chopper muttered. "Fire ain't."

Tyrell hammered the bag harder, as if trying to drown out the conversation.

"He ain't been hit yet," Mickey said.

"Then maybe you help with that," Chopper replied.

Mickey grunted.

"Or maybe I drink my coffee and mind my business."

Chopper held Mickey's gaze for a long, knowing moment.

"He reminds you of you."

Mickey didn't need to answer. The truth sat heavy in the air between them.

"Difference is," Chopper added, "you came in here looking for something. He ain't looking. He's running."

Mickey watched Tyrell one more time—the hunger, the speed, the beautiful recklessness—and something old in him shifted.

Recognition, maybe.

Or the ghost of purpose.

* * *

The fight against Julio Delgado was held at Atlantic City in 1999. The air in the ballroom reeked of cheap cologne, old cigars, and desperation.

Mickey Brannigan sat in his corner between the second and third rounds, breathing through his mouth, blood trickling from his nostril into the corner of his lips.

Delgado was twenty-seven. Undefeated. Fast hands. He was everything Mickey used to be—and everything he wasn't anymore. Mickey was slower, older. No longer fighting for glory, just survival. A paycheck. One more gasp of relevance.

Delgado came out in the third round, as if he knew it was the last chapter of a once compelling story. Jab to the body, right to the temple, left hook to the liver. Mickey backed up, his legs refusing to cooperate. Every synapse in his brain told him to move, to fire back—but the body didn't listen anymore.

He caught a right uppercut flush on the chin and folded in the center of the ring. The ref didn't even bother counting.

And just like that, it was over.

They took him to the hospital after. Concussion. Cracked rib. Orbital swelling.

But the worst part wasn't the pain. It was the silence. No reporters waited.

No fans lingered. No cameras. No headlines. Just an empty hallway and a hospital bill.

He lay in bed staring at the ceiling tiles, tasting the metallic sting of blood in the back of his throat. Tried to tell himself it was just a bad night. That he still had something left. But even that lie had gotten tired.

The next morning, he watched Delgado, smiling in a suit, thanking Mickey for "giving me my first real test."

He often thought about Delgado. About the loneliness after the lights went out. About how no one told him how fast it all ends.

Mickey had made his peace with being forgotten.

But as he watched Tyrell, he felt something he hadn't felt in years—the faintest hint of purpose gnawing its way back into his chest.

Maybe—just maybe—through Tyrell, he could still be remembered.

3

Voices from the Past

The bell above the door gave a tired little jingle as Mickey stepped into the South Boston Sports Memorabilia Shop. A bite of cold followed him inside before the door swung shut.

The place hadn't changed. Still cramped, still cluttered with signed baseballs sealed in yellowing plastic, framed Bruins uniforms and fight posters curling under their glass—warriors frozen in time, most of them long buried.

Behind the counter stood Phil Sanders—wearing a sweatshirt that must've survived twenty winters. He looked up, ready to give the standard customer greeting.

Recognition hit him like a slow sunrise.

"Jesus… Mick Brannigan."

Mickey offered the faintest smile.

"Hey, Phil. Been a while. Place looks good."

They met halfway across the counter, shaking hands—familiar, but with an awkwardness edged by years neither of them said aloud.

"You back around for good?" Phil asked.

"Just passing through."

Phil nodded, polite but uncertain. "You look good."

"You always were a bad liar."

Phil barked out a laugh—genuine, then fading as he took in Mickey's thin frame, the shadows under his eyes, the bones showing through the face that once drew crowds.

"How's the wife and kids?" Mickey asked.

Phil scratched the back of his neck. "Divorced now. Kids are alright. Debbie took all my money."

Mickey winced softly. "I was wondering…. you still do those signings? Gloves, photos—whatever you got. I could sit for a couple hours"

Phil's face fell before he could hide it.

"Ah… I don't know, Mick. Kids today barely know Hagler, never mind us dinosaurs. I just don't think it'd move much."

The blow landed clean. Mickey didn't show it.

"Yeah. No worries. Figured I'd ask."

For a moment, they stood in the narrow shop surrounded by framed legends—men who mattered once and now only to collectors and ghosts.

Phil gestured toward a photo on the wall.

Mickey and Maria, young and bright under the Garden lights, smiling like they'd beaten the whole world.

"Those were good nights," Phil said quietly.

"Yeah," Mickey murmured. "They were something."

Silence settled—soft, heavy.

"Good seeing you, Phil," Mickey whispered.

Phil nodded, sensing the line Mickey couldn't cross.

"Well… it's good seeing you, Mick. Don't be a stranger."

Mickey tried on a small grin. "Yeah, well… I guess I'm a little stranger than I used to be."

He turned toward the door.

A voice exploded behind him.

"MICKEY BRANNIGAN!"

Mickey froze. The voice was ragged but thunderous, as if someone had announced a prizefight to a crowd of one. He turned. There, crossing the street in a tattered Celtics jacket, gym shorts, and socks pulled high above white sneakers, was a man with a greasy mop of hair and a handlebar mustache. Mid-sixties, wiry, bug-eyed, and carrying a folded newspaper in one hand and a thermos in the other.

He approached like a man on a mission… or one on parole.

"You're Mickey 'The Brick' Brannigan!" Arlo shouted. "The South End Sledgehammer! The Irish Executioner!"

Mickey sighed. "They just call me Mickey these days."

"Boston Garden! October '86! You knocked out Castillo with that inside right like he owed you money!"

"Guess that's how I assembled all those nicknames."

"I can't believe it. You're alive."

Arlo's bag hit the floor—apples rolling everywhere. He fumbled in his wallet, dropping receipts, fortune-cookie slips, an old subway pass.

"You gotta sign something. Anything. You got a pen?"

"Do I look like a man who carries pens?"

"You're a writer of pain, Mickey! Sign my arm!"

"I'm not signing your arm."

"I'll get it tattooed!"

"It'll look ridiculous."

"Do I look like I care?"

Mickey stared up at the clear sky, exhaled, then surrendered.

"Fine. Give me something."

Arlo thrust a yellow parking ticket into his hand.

"That'll do," Mickey muttered.

Arlo vibrated with joy.

"My cousin is gonna crap his pants! He said you died in Atlantic City with a bottle of Jack and a waitress named Rhonda."

Mickey's smile dimmed a fraction. "Thanks. Means more than you know."

"If you ever need a hype man, I work cheap."

"I'll keep you in mind."

"I'll fight someone for you right now."

Arlo threw a wild, lurching combination that nearly sent him into a mailbox.

"Don't hurt yourself," Mickey said.

"Never been knocked out!"

"You ever been hit?"

"Nope!"

"Makes sense."

Mickey descended the steps toward the train, chuckling despite himself.

Behind him, Arlo kept shouting:

"MICK! I LOVE YOU! YOU'RE A DAMN LEGEND! BRANNIGAN FOREVER!!"

* * *

Mickey Brannigan had always told himself he didn't care what people thought.

It was a lie.

From the first time he stepped into a ring as a kid fighting smokers in dingy halls, he'd felt it—that invisible pull between himself and the people in the stands. The claps, the shouts, the way strangers' faces lit up when he landed a clean shot. He fed on it. Lived for it.

They were more than just "the crowd" to him. They were his proof. Proof he wasn't just some loudmouth from Southie with a bad temper and fists he didn't know what to do with. Every cheer told him he mattered, that the work meant something.

And that's why 1989 never stopped haunting him.

He could still see it. Bright lights of the arena. His name echoing in the rafters as he walked to the ring with the belt snug around his waist. He'd looked up at the upper decks, at the families and the kids with homemade signs, and thought, *I can't lose tonight.*

By the seventh round, he knew he was in trouble. His legs felt heavy, the other guy— young, hungry—kept pressing, finding gaps Mickey couldn't close. In the tenth, a left hook caught him clean, and he went down. He got up, but the fight was already gone.

The ref raised the kid's hand, the crowd roared—but it wasn't for Mickey.

In the locker room afterward, the press swarmed, microphones shoved in his face, but all Mickey could think about were the fans who'd believed in him. He imagined them on the train ride home, telling each other it was time to root for someone else.

It was the first time in his career he felt he'd let them down.

* * *

The car now rattled over the Zakim Bridge, Mickey's knuckles gripping the steering wheel. South Boston faded behind him, replaced by highways that stretched into the well-trimmed edges of suburban comfort. Strip malls gave way to Colonial homes with basketball hoops and fancy mailboxes.

Mickey arrived in Lexington. It didn't just look different. It breathed different. The air was cleaner here—less smoke, more mulch and magnolias. The roads didn't scream, they hummed. Sidewalks were smooth. Fences white. And the dogs—they were walked, not fought.

Mickey slowed near a rotary flanked by American flags and well-maintained hedges. It all felt like a postcard of a world he never mailed himself into.

He found Jackie's place on a quiet side street. A wind chime rang out as he approached the front steps. It sounded like wind through glass.

He knocked once. The door opened a moment later to reveal Jackie Brannigan.

She was eight years younger, born in the dead of winter during a blizzard that shut down all of South Boston. Mickey remembered sitting in the hospital waiting room with a vending machine hot chocolate, his feet barely touching the floor, when his father came out and told him, "It's a girl."

Jacqueline Marie Brannigan.

He didn't know it then, but from that moment forward, he would never not feel responsible for her.

Their mother worked double shifts and their father was tough as nails—proud and not always gentle with words. So it fell to Mickey, even as a boy, to be Jackie's protector.

When she was scared of the dark, he'd leave his door cracked open. When she had a nightmare, he was the one who sat on the floor beside her bed until she fell back asleep.

He walked her to elementary school when he was in high school. He was her hero, and she was the only person Mickey ever allowed to see the soft parts of him.

But when their father died in 1976, everything changed.

Grief hit their family like a wrecking ball. Their mother unraveled slowly—numbed by grief, crushed by bills—and Mickey had no choice but to step up. He became more than her big brother. He became her second father.

He made her breakfast before school, helped her with homework, taught her how to throw a punch, just in case. If she got sick, he skipped work to take care of her.

And Jackie loved him for it—until she didn't.

It was 2001. Mickey was washed up and aching in places he didn't talk about. His best fighting days were behind him, but he was still clinging to the shell of who he used to be.

Jackie brought a new boyfriend around. Mike. Some smarmy bartender who wore sunglasses indoors and called Mickey "Champ" like it was a joke.

At first, Mickey tried to be civil. But it didn't take long to see the signs—Mike wasn't just disrespectful. He was mean. Controlling. Mickey caught a bruise on Jackie's wrist one night at dinner and lost it.

He showed up at Mike's apartment unannounced. No words. Just fists.

By the time it was over, Mickey's knuckles were broken and Mike had three cracked ribs and a fractured jaw. Mickey got arrested but didn't spend any time inside. Old favors got called in. Rumor on the street was that Chopper called in some favors with the police.

The next year, Mickey packed what little he had left and left Boston. He moved to Arizona. A place with no history, no shadows, and no Jackie. They didn't speak for nearly five years.

The door opened after a pause. Jackie Brannigan stood there.

"Jesus Christ," she whispered.

"Hey, Jackie." Mickey tried to smile, though it barely held. "Just in the neighborhood."

"I can't believe it."

"You expecting a client?" he asked.

"A contractor. You're not drywall."

"Nah," Mickey muttered. "Just the cracks behind it."

She stared at him a moment longer, then sighed and stepped aside. "Come in before the neighbors think I'm hiding a fugitive."

"Want me to take my shoes off? Place looks spotless."

"No. Just come in, Mick."

The inside of Jackie's home was warm, inviting. Bookshelves lined the walls. The scent of chamomile tea lingered in the air, faint but steady.

It was the kind of home Mickey might've had in another life.

Jackie walked ahead into the kitchen. She poured coffee, watching him carefully from across the counter. Worry and curiosity shifted across her face. She returned with two mugs, handing him one before sitting opposite.

"You haven't been in the neighborhood in over ten years," she said.

"Yeah. It's been a long time."

"You look like shit."

Mickey gave a small laugh, coughing through it. "That's what Chopper said."

A beat of silence hung between them.

"You still know how to make a good cup of coffee," Mickey said softly, looking to change the subject.

"After all this time, why are you here, Mick?"

"I don't know. Maybe just some unfinished business."

"Oh, come on. You didn't even come to Mom's funeral."

"I was in Reno," he said quickly. "Thought I'd mess it up if I showed."

"You always think that. So you don't show up and still mess it up."

Jackie watched him carefully, her voice lowering. "After all these years, you finally decide to come back. The question is why? Are you dying?"

He didn't answer. His eyes shifted toward the window, where the wind stirred the chimes.

"I know that face," she said, her voice tightening. "What is it?"

"Pancreas," Mickey said finally. His tone was flat, but his eyes gave him away. "Doc says it's going to be quick. Offered chemo to drag it out. I said no."

Her eyes darkened. "So when did you find out?"

"Couple weeks ago. Figured I was just tired. But being tired doesn't creep into your bones like this."

She sat back, arms crossed, hurt flickering across her features. "And you have told nobody?"

"No. And I didn't come for pity."

"You should have come sooner. Disappearing isn't mercy, Mick. It's lazy and selfish."

He nodded, the words sinking into him. "Probably."

Silence again, heavy, filled only by the hum of the refrigerator.

"I was scared," Mickey admitted. "Not of dying—of what it meant."

Jackie shook her head. "You fight everything. People. Feelings. You don't know how to lay anything down."

"I just don't want to go without making peace. With Danny. With… everything."

"And you're staying in Boston?"

"For now. Crashing at Chopper's Gym. Sleeping next to a stack of old Everlast bags and a broken rowing machine."

"You could've asked me."

"No. That's not the way this goes."

"Why?" she pressed.

"'Cause I didn't think I had the right."

"And now?"

"Now I don't have the time to keep being a coward."

She let that hang between them, her eyes softening but her jaw firm.

"Be ready for Danny not to want anything to do with you," she said finally.

"I am. But I gotta try."

Jackie leaned forward, softer now. "You hurt a lot of people, Mickey. But you were hurting too. You never let anyone help."

"Fighters don't ask for help."

"Maybe it's time you let someone pick you up."

He nodded slowly, eyes glistening.

"Let me talk to him," Jackie offered. "Ease him into it."

"Nah. That ain't fair. I broke it. I gotta try to fix it myself."

"Then let me help in the other way. Stay here. At least for a few days."

Mickey chuckled, shaking his head. "Lexington's too clean for me. But thanks."

The two of them shared a silence. Then Mickey stood, stretching his sore back until it popped.

"Well," he said, forcing a smile, "I'll let you get back to your drywall."

"Mick—" Jackie's voice cracked.

He turned at the door.

"Wish I came back sooner," he said quietly.

"Me too." Her voice carried the pain she'd hidden for years.

"I love you," Jackie said. "Despite… everything."

"That's your biggest flaw, kid," Mickey murmured. "Too much heart."

"Maybe. But you used to have one too."

He looked at her one last time, deeply, as if memorizing her face. Then he nodded and stepped out into the fading light.

Outside the window, a breeze picked up, brushing through the chimes. And for a moment, he didn't feel like a dying man or a disgraced fighter. Just a brother, wishing he'd come sooner.

4

The Son

The whiteboard marker squeaked faintly as Daniel Brannigan, 38, underlined the words *The Gilded Age* in block letters. His handwriting was clean, deliberate.

Danny Brannigan carried himself as if someone who had spent his whole life learning how not to take up space. He had the quiet manner of a man used to listening more than speaking, and a patience that came less from wisdom than from years of disappointment.

As a boy, though, Danny had been different. He'd been a shadow that followed every step his father made, a wide-eyed kid perched on the ring apron at Chopper's Gym, swinging his little legs while watching Mickey spar. He never cared if his father was facing a top contender or some random sparring partner—Danny thought he was watching Superman.

At home, though, it was Maria who anchored him. He was a mama's boy through and through, leaning on her when Mickey was gone on the road or too broken down to notice what his son needed. Maria was the one who made sure Danny's homework was finished, his scraped knees were cleaned, and his fears soothed in the quiet of the night. But even then, even in her warmth, Danny's heart tilted toward his father. He worshiped Mickey in the way only a boy can worship a man who doesn't always deserve it.

And then came the years that cracked that worship apart. The drinking. The losing. The nights when Mickey stumbled through the door, smelling of sweat and whiskey, too angry at himself to speak, too proud to apologize. Danny learned quickly that his father was no invincible Superman.

He loved him anyway. That was the hardest part. Danny never stopped wanting to believe. Even now, all these years later, with Mickey gone from his life and silence stretching wider than memory, Danny carried the ghost of that boyhood worship like a scar.

The room was quiet—not with boredom but with respect. Twenty-five high school juniors sat upright at their desks, notebooks open, phones stashed away without reminders. It wasn't fear that held the room steady. It was something else—something rarer in a high school classroom. It was command.

Danny turned, resting the marker against the edge of the board. His blue oxford shirt was rolled at the sleeves, tie loosened slightly. He didn't dress to impress, but he wore authority the way some men wore armor.

"Who can tell me what made the Gilded Age gilded?" he asked, eyes scanning the rows.

A girl near the window raised her hand. "Because it looked shiny on the outside, but underneath it was corrupt?"

Danny nodded, impressed. "Exactly. Gilded means coated in gold—not solid gold. The surface sparkled, but inside, you had child labor, brutal poverty, political machines. The illusion of greatness, built on cracks."

He clicked the black remote and a photo of a 19th century tenement flashed on the screen.

"It looked like progress. But it was survival. Day by day. And no matter how many bricks they stacked, some cracks were too wide to fix."

One student, a sharp-eyed boy in the front row, tilted his head. Danny smiled and changed the slide.

"Homework: read chapters 11 through 13. But more importantly," he added, "think about what our society coats in gold today."

Danny exhaled. Slow. Controlled. He wiped the board clean with firm, even strokes. Each swipe erased more than ink. It erased thought. History. Weight. Only when he finished did he lean against the edge of his desk, gazing out the window.

He was nothing like Mickey Brannigan. He had built his life from structure, not fire. From classrooms, not rings. From quiet mornings and lesson plans, not from sweat, blood, and pride.

Danny sat alone at his desk after the last bell. His eyes lingered on a framed photo near the corner—not of his own family, but a black-and-white shot of Theodore Roosevelt addressing a crowd.

History. Men of words and action.

He reached into the bottom drawer, pulled out a small, worn shoe-box. Inside: old programs, clippings, a folded ticket stub yellowed with time. On top was a Polaroid—blurry, but still vivid in memory.

Danny touched it, thumb brushing the corner. And just like that—the present faded.

October 1986

The noise outside the locker room was a living thing. It pulsed through the concrete walls, a raw mix of cheers and foot stomps, a stadium of euphoria trying to push its way into the small, musty room backstage.

Mickey Brannigan sat hunched forward on a wooden bench, elbows on knees, towel draped over his head. His bare torso gleamed with sweat and liniment oil. A fresh welt bloomed along his ribs. His right hand trembled slightly, still wrapped in red-stained tape.

But beside him, gleaming under the flickering overhead bulb, sat the Middleweight Championship belt. He hadn't just survived. He had won.

Across the room stood Maria—radiant, a woman who never quite looked as if she belonged in a boxing locker room. She wore a simple white blouse and jeans, her hair pulled back loosely, strands sticking to her cheek in the humid air.

And beside her, bouncing on his heels, was a boy of four with the kind of electric joy that only a child could possess.

Danny darted across the room, arms wide, hoodie sleeves dragging past his fingertips, and threw himself into his father's lap.

"You did it, Dad!" he squealed. "You're the champion of the whole world!"

Mickey chuckled as he caught him, wincing slightly from bruised ribs but smiling big.

"Damn right I did," Mickey said, pulling the towel off his head and tossing it aside.

"I told everyone at school you would!" Danny beamed, gripping the over sized belt that rested beside them on the bench.

"Did you now?"

"Yup!" Danny nodded. "I told them you were the strongest guy on the planet!"

Mickey looked over at Maria, who crossed her arms and smirked, amusement dancing behind tired eyes.

"You're raising a real hype man," she said.

"He's gonna get me in trouble with the promoters," Mickey joked, running a gloved hand gently across Danny's head. "Might have to start paying him."

The belt glinted in the light. The blood on Mickey's knuckles began to dry. And for that one night—that one perfect, impossible night—Mickey Brannigan was everything a son could believe in.

Danny, now back in present time, sat with the photo between his fingers, his thumb brushing gently along the edge as if trying to press the image deeper into memory. He didn't smile. Not exactly. But there was something soft in his eyes. Regret. Longing. Maybe both.

He placed the photo back into the box carefully, almost reverently, and closed the lid. The box returned to the drawer. Out of sight, but never really gone.

He stood and walked slowly toward the window. Outside, the wind moved through the trees with lazy ease. Students crossed the quad without urgency. The world went on.

Danny pressed his hand against the glass. That boy in the locker room...

That boy was still in there somewhere. Just harder to find.

* * *

The cold crisp air inside the rink bit through Danny's jacket as he stepped inside. The familiar scent of cold rubber, Zamboni fuel, and popcorn hit him like an old song.

He spotted Caleb immediately—number 17, navy jersey, skating like a blur across the ice, already taller than he had any right to be at eleven.

Danny stood behind, hands in his coat pockets, watching. Caleb intercepted a pass and fired a wrist shot into the upper corner of the net.

"You missed the first period."

The voice came from his left—familiar, soft, and sharper than it used to be.

Danny turned. It was Lena. Same posture. Same almond eyes, only more tired now.

"Traffic," Danny said. "And a last-minute meeting."

Lena raised a brow. "There's always traffic."

They stood in silence for a few moments, watching Caleb skate backward into defensive position, directing his teammates with pointed fingers and sharp eyes.

"He looks good out there," Danny said.

"He is," she replied. "He's been working harder. Wants to make the elite team this spring."

The horn buzzed to end the period. Caleb skated toward the bench, pulling off his helmet, revealing sweat-matted hair and the Brannigan jawline. He looked up toward the stands. His eyes scanned, and for a moment they locked.

Danny stood there, alone again, watching his son skate out for the next period—a boy already carving his own path.

The hockey game ended in a win. Danny never stayed long after the final buzzer.

Back in his car, parked just outside the rink, the world felt quiet again. Too quiet. The kind that presses on your chest when the memories start crawling back, uninvited.

He sat behind the wheel. The photograph he kept tucked in the sun visor was still there—his mother, Maria, beaming in the late '80s, holding a much younger Danny on her lap. The smile on her face was effortless. Her eyes made everything feel okay.

Danny touched the corner of the photo with his fingertip. His voice barely above a whisper.

"Hey, Mom."

She was the one person who had always believed in him. Not because he was special, but because she made him feel safe. In a world defined by Mickey's highs and lows, Maria had been the steady center. A gentle but strong woman who held the family together with simple things: evening dinners, quiet hugs, handwritten notes in his backpack on test days.

And then there was that year—1992.

His mother had gone to the hospital. She'd been glowing, hopeful. They'd all talked about the new baby. Danny was going to be a big brother. He remembered touching her belly, whispering stories to it at night. He remembered Mickey even talking about cutting back on traveling to be home more.

And then, just like that, it was gone.

He didn't understand the word *miscarriage* at the time. No one explained much. Just that his mom came home different—quieter, eyes sometimes farther away.

Mickey didn't handle it well. The gym became home more than the house did.

Danny remembered lying in bed at night hearing them argue in low voices, words slipping under the door like smoke. His mother trying to reach him, and Mickey always just out of reach.

It was the beginning of the unraveling.

Maria never blamed anyone. Never once. But Danny remembered her once sitting beside him on the porch swing in early fall, watching the leaves scatter across the lawn.

"You know what I prayed for?" she had asked softly.

He'd shaken his head.

"A daughter. I was going to name her Grace."

Danny had reached for her hand.

"Do you still pray?"

Maria had smiled, just a little. "I do. But these days, I just hope."

That moment—that quiet admission—stayed with him. Not the tragedy, but the tenderness. The way she never let bitterness win.

And now, with her gone all these years, it was Maria's memory—not Mickey's legacy— that shaped the man he became.

He started the car and stared straight ahead.

There was still a boy inside him who wished she could've seen him now—leading classrooms, raising a son of his own. There was still a part of him that thought she was the only one who truly understood the storm Mickey carried around in his chest.

He missed her every day.

5

Young Fire

Tyrell found his grandmother Evelyn in the small room at the end of the corridor, sitting by the window in her familiar chair.

An old black-and-white western flickered on the television, cowboys riding across a landscape she once would've narrated beat by beat. Now she stared past it.

She turned as Tyrell stepped in.

"You here about the laundry?" she asked, smiling like it was the most natural thing in the world.

Tyrell swallowed, gently. "Yeah," he said. "Laundry."

She nodded toward a neatly folded towel on the bed—one of the last tasks she still "assigned" to him in her slipstream of memories. He didn't correct her. Correction only bruised the moment and made her confusion worse.

He sat beside her, careful not to startle her, careful not to hope for recognition.

"You doing okay today?" he asked.

"The birds were loud this morning," she said thoughtfully. Then her voice drifted, losing the thread. "But… I like the sound."

Her hand found his—not with intention, not with clarity, but with some leftover muscle memory of a thousand afternoons she'd once spent raising him. For a heartbeat her eyes sharpened. They almost saw him.

Almost.

"You here to bring the lunch?" she asked.

"They already brought it, Grandma."

She nodded, fading again, drifting back into the fog.

"Well whoever is working that kitchen," she muttered, "should start thinking about a new line of work."

Tyrell let a small grin tug at his mouth. "You always were a tough critic."

"No flavor," she said, offended on principle.

He just sat with her after that—no noise, no need to speak, simply sharing space the way people do when words fail them.

"I'm right here, Grandma," he whispered.

She slid a cup of orange Jell-O toward him, her hand tiny, shaking. "Eat it," she said. "I don't want it going to waste."

* * *

Tyrell pushed through the doors and stepped into the cold. He didn't cry. He didn't break. He simply rested his hands on his hips, drew in a long breath, and steadied himself. Grief for him wasn't a storm—it was a weight, one he carried silently, like another set of gloves in his bag.

He reached into his jacket pocket and pulled out the Jell-O cup she'd given him. A nurse passing by offered a gentle "Evening."

He nodded back.

Standing there in the parking lot, he peeled back the foil and ate the Jell-O with the small plastic spoon he kept in his pocket from gas-station dinners. He didn't care for the taste. But she'd given it to him. That mattered.

* * *

The apartment felt smaller every time he walked into it.

Malik, eight years old and stubbornly focused, sat at the kitchen table doing homework with a pencil that had been sharpened down to a stub.

Tyrell set a grocery bag on the counter. "Got something for dinner."

His mother Angela stirred a thin pot on the stove, steam rising into the cold light. She didn't turn.

Tyrell placed a few apples on the table and slid one toward Malik.

"For you, little man."

The kid's face brightened like someone had handed him treasure. Angela glanced over, her expression unreadable.

"You were supposed to be at the GED center this morning," she said.

"Gym ran long."

"Gym always runs long."

This time she turned—wiping her hands on a faded rag, eyes taking him in with that mixture of disappointment and worry mothers perfect over time.

"You think fighting is the answer to everything?" she asked.

He didn't respond. He didn't have a lie that wouldn't offend her or a truth that wouldn't wound them both.

"Your daddy had hands too," she said.

The words landed hard enough to echo in the cramped kitchen.

Tyrell steadied himself.

"I ain't him," he said quietly.

She didn't confirm or deny it. She just turned back to the stove.

"The heat bill came," she said. "They're threatening to shut it again."

Tyrell opened his mouth, then closed it—the admission of failure stinging more than any punch he'd taken.

She didn't face him, but her stirring slowed.

Malik watched them both, wide-eyed, absorbing the world he was growing into.

"I'm trying" Tyrell murmured.

"I know," she said softly.

A beat.

"Try harder."

It wasn't harsh. It was the truth she lived with.

Tyrell slung his gym bag over his shoulder, pausing at the door.

"Love you, Ma."

She didn't turn, but her voice cracked just enough to betray her heart.

"Get to your class tomorrow."

He nodded once and slipped out.

* * *

His bedroom was barely a room. Tyrell sat on the edge of the mattress, unwrapping tape from his hands. His knuckles were raw; his shoulders ached in ways he didn't allow himself to admit.

His phone buzzed on the bed. Screen cracked, battery showing 9%.

He leaned back, catching his breath. For a moment he just sat there in the half-dark, the faint hum of traffic outside filling the silence. Then he reached for his cracked phone, the screen smeared and spider-veined from a drop months ago. He opened YouTube and typed the name that had been on his mind.

Mickey Brannigan.

The video buffered, the grainy image of the arena filling the small screen. Tyrell turned the phone sideways and rested it against his knee. There was Mickey, decades younger, gloves taped tight, bouncing on the balls of his feet like the canvas itself belonged to him. His shoulders rolled loose, his chin tucked, his whole presence humming with menace and purpose.

Tyrell leaned forward, studying every twitch of Mickey's body, every feint, every snap of the jab. He knew this fight—Brannigan's war against Castillo, the one that people still talked about—but he watched it like it was brand new. Mickey ate a shot to land one harder, absorbed punishment with that granite chin, and came forward again and again until the other man wilted.

Tyrell's chest rose and fell with the rhythm of the bout. His knuckles flexed, fists curling unconsciously. He whispered under his breath, almost like a prayer.

"That's how you do it."

The crowd roared through the tinny speaker, drowning his room in the sound of glory. Tyrell shut his eyes, letting it sink into him—the idea that somewhere, maybe, he had the same steel in his blood.

When the knockout came—Mickey's right hand crashing home like a hammer—Tyrell exhaled sharply, like he'd thrown it himself. He sat back, the glow of the phone screen painting his face.

One day, he thought. *One day they'll be chanting my name.*

He dropped to the floor without thinking, palms pressing into the cold linoleum. His arms strained as he began to pump out push ups. The muscles in his shoulders and chest burned, but he welcomed the fire.

When his arms finally gave out, he pushed himself onto his knees, sweat dripping down his back. He got to his feet and moved to the cracked mirror hanging over his dresser. His reflection looked back at him.

For the first time in a long time, he didn't just see a kid stuck in the projects with no future to speak of. He saw someone who could step into a ring and make people take notice. Someone who, maybe, could carry his family somewhere better.

Tyrell touched the glass with the tips of his fingers, almost as if trying to connect with the man in the mirror. His lips curved, not quite a smile, but something close.

"This is my time."

<h1 style="text-align:center">6</h1>

Bottom of the Canvas

Darkness.

Mickey Brannigan stood in the center of a ring drenched in light. Sweat poured off him. The canvas beneath his boots was soaked with blood, and the ropes looked a mile away.

Across from him stood a man half his age—Carlos "El Machete" Corte, the young lion who was a top prospect in the mid-1990s.

In the dream, Corte looked larger than life—wide shoulders and perfect footwork.

The crowd was roaring. Or maybe laughing. He couldn't tell anymore.

Corte slipped a jab. Threw a left hook.

Mickey tried to move. His legs wouldn't fire. He felt stuck in cement.

The punch landed flush on his temple. Then another. And another.

The ref didn't stop it. The bell never rang.

Mickey's body crumpled to the mat in slow motion, but the sound was deafening. He looked up from the canvas and saw the one face that truly broke him: Danny.

Just a boy. Standing ringside with Maria. Both of them watching, horrified. Danny reached for him. Maria turned away.

Mickey screamed—

He jolted upright on the thin mattress, soaked in sweat and gasping for breath. The gym was silent around him.

He swung his legs over the side of the cot. His stomach twisted violently. He tried to breathe through it, but the pain came like a blade to the gut.

His hands clutched his abdomen.

"Jesus—"

He stumbled out of the room, down the narrow hallway toward the staff bathroom.

He gripped the sink. Pale. Lips cracked. He looked like the ghost of the man in that old poster on the gym wall.

Then he lurched toward the toilet and vomited.

There was blood in it. Not a lot. But enough.

He sat on the cold tile, back against the wall, breathing in shallow rasps. His body trembled.

Eventually, the pain eased into a low ache. His head lolled back, staring at the ceiling.

Mickey closed his eyes again.

Corte. That fight. It wasn't just about the loss. It was what it symbolized.

Back then, he told himself he stayed down because his body gave out.

But the truth?

He stayed down because he no longer knew how to get back up.

* * *

"You look like hell," Chopper said. "Nightmares?"

Mickey nodded, slow. "Why the hell didn't you throw in the towel?"

Chopper didn't answer right away. He took a long sip from his mug.

"I mean, seriously," Mickey pressed. "You saw it. I was a walking heavy bag. You let me eat shots for six rounds."

"Because you begged me not to," Chopper said finally.

Mickey's laugh was bitter, hollow. "I was begging for something, Chop. You were supposed to know better than I did."

"You think I didn't know you were done? I knew by the time you were lacing up. But if I'd thrown that towel… you'd have never spoken to me again."

"Maybe I shouldn't have," Mickey muttered.

"Maybe I should've thrown it," Chopper countered. "But then what? You'd have limped out of that ring screaming betrayal. You wouldn't have retired. You'd have booked another fight just to prove I was wrong."

Mickey rubbed a hand over his face. "Maybe I needed someone to betray me. Instead, I just… faded. Until nobody gave a shit anymore."

The silence between them grew heavy.

"You think it didn't kill me, watching you go down like that?" Chopper asked, voice low.

Mickey's jaw tightened. "I see Danny in the dream. Watching me get knocked out. He's always walking away."

"He did walk away," Chopper said. "But not because you lost. Because you disappeared. There's a difference."

"Yeah." Mickey's voice was barely more than a whisper. "I know that now. Too late."

"Maybe. Maybe not."

Mickey looked down at his hands, scarred and swollen from years of punishment. "He's got a kid now. I saw them once. Didn't say a word."

"Then say it now," Chopper said firmly.

Mickey lifted his eyes. "What's that?"

"Sorry."

Mickey leaned back in the chair, staring up at the single light above the ring. "I'm tired, Chop."

After the loss to Corte, the press had tried to ask a lot of questions, but he'd just walked past them. His face was swollen, jaw tight. His ribs screamed every time he breathed.

But that wasn't the pain that lingered.

The worst pain was deeper.

"You let it all slip through your fingers", he would often say to himself.

* * *

Morning settled slowly into Chopper's Gym.

Tyrell moved through the space with the restless energy of someone who didn't know how to be still. His jump rope cut the air in tight, fast slaps; sweat dotted the floor beneath him like punctuation marks.

Across the room, Mickey sat on a folding chair.

"You keep going like that," Mickey muttered without looking up, "gonna wear out the paint."

Tyrell grinned and let the rope fall, grabbing a towel to wipe his face.

"Watched your fight with Castillo last night," he said, breath still quick.

"Didn't think you were the type to go toe-to-toe that long."

"Didn't think either," Mickey replied. "That was my problem."

Tyrell laughed, dropped onto the bench across from him, elbows on his knees. He let the silence stretch just enough to feel like a question.

"What's it like?" Tyrell asked quietly. "The top?"

Mickey finished a wrap, pulled it tight.

"Short," he said.

Tyrell nodded like he already knew that, but needed to hear it anyway.

"Why'd you keep fighting after?" he asked.

Mickey didn't look up.

"Didn't know how to do much else."

A quiet settled between them—not uncomfortable, but honest.

"You ever get scared?" Tyrell asked.

Mickey snorted. "If you're not scared, you're not alive."

Tyrell let his eyes drift toward the ring.

"Chopper always said fear sharpens you."

"Fear keeps you honest," Mickey said.

There was something in his tone—something that had nothing to do with boxing—and Tyrell caught it. He studied Mickey's face, the lines etched by old blows and older regrets.

"You think I got it?" Tyrell asked.

Mickey finally met his eyes.

"You're fast," he said. "Clean. But you haven't been hit by someone who doesn't care yet."

Tyrell smirked.

"You offering?"

"Kid, I'm offering nothing," Mickey said, leaning back. "You want to learn, that's on you."

Tyrell nodded, absorbing the weight of that. A truth, delivered plainly.

"Never really had anyone tell me the truth before," Tyrell said, voice low.

Mickey watched him for a long moment.

"Alright," he said at last. "Truth one—your left side's Christmas morning. Wide open. Truth two—you breathe like you're showing off."

Tyrell laughed, shaking his head.

"You talk like a father," he said.

Mickey froze—the smallest shift, barely visible, but it hit the air like a dropped glove.

"Used to be," he said quietly.

Tyrell looked down at his shoes, the humor draining, replaced by something heavier.

"My grandma used to say the ring teaches you things nobody else can," he murmured.

"It teaches you things," Mickey said.

He paused, voice softening.

"Doesn't teach you everything."

They sat in the dim gym light—two men surrounded by bags and benches and the echoes of past rounds—saying more than the words they spoke, each hearing something they needed even if they didn't admit it.

7

It Starts Now

Tyrell cracked eggs over a pan, one-handed, like he'd learned out of necessity more than skill. Kiesha sat at the table scrolling on a cracked phone, her face lit by the shifting glow of something she couldn't load because the Wi-Fi kept cutting out. Malik drummed with two pencils, humming off-beat, lost in a world he invented.

"The Wi-Fi's trash again," Kiesha muttered. "Every time Ma's not here, it cuts out."

"That's 'cause she didn't pay it," Tyrell said, flipping the eggs. "Chill."

Malik looked up, the pencils stilled.

"So when you gonna be rich, Ty?"

Tyrell snorted. "What you mean?"

"You keep saying boxing gonna get us out."

Tyrell plated the eggs and set them in front of his siblings. Sat down with his own plate, tired but trying to hide it.

"I'm working on it," he said.

"Working?" Kiesha scoffed. "You ain't even got a job."

"I do," Tyrell said. "Just not the kind with a name tag."

Kiesha shook her head. "Nah. What you do is hit a bag till your knuckles split. That ain't paying rent."

Tyrell stared at her, jaw tightening.

"I ain't just hitting a bag. I'm training."

"With who?" Malik asked, leaning forward.

Tyrell sat back, voice casual—but the pride underneath betrayed him.

"With Mickey Brannigan."

Kiesha frowned. "Who's that?"

"Former champ," Tyrell said. "Chopper's got his poster on the wall."

Malik's face lit up. "For real? You training with a world champ?"

Kiesha rolled her eyes. "He's old, Ty. What's an old dude gonna teach you?"

Tyrell hesitated, then leaned in a bit.

"Plenty."

She didn't believe him—but she didn't argue either.

"Look," he said, softer now, "I know you think I'm wasting time. But he's showing me things nobody else ever did."

Malik threw little punches in his seat. "You gonna be on ESPN?"

"One day," Tyrell said.

"Or you'll end up like him," Kiesha murmured.

Tyrell stared down at his plate, jaw locked.

"Maybe," he said. "But at least I'm trying for something."

Kiesha went quiet. Chewed slowly. Didn't admit she respected that—but she didn't have to.

"I don't care what happens to me," Tyrell said, watching them both. "Long as you two don't gotta grow up the way I did."

Kiesha finally looked at him, eyes sharper than her tone.

"Then don't get yourself killed trying. We need you."

"I'm not going anywhere," Tyrell said.

The words hung in the kitchen like a promise he needed to believe just as much as they did.

* * *

A thin morning fog drifted over the rows of abandoned cars like a ghost undecided about who to haunt. Rusted hoods gleamed dully under the pale sun, and somewhere overhead a seagull screamed—the kind of sound that made cold mornings feel colder.

Tyrell walked cautiously between piles of scrap metal, bundled in a hoodie still damp from yesterday's sweat.

"You sure this is the right address?" he asked the empty yard.

A voice cut through from behind a half-crushed pickup truck.

"You're late."

Tyrell turned. Mickey emerged with a coffee in one hand and a towel slung over his shoulder.

"It's six fifty-nine," Tyrell said.

"That's late in my world."

Tyrell looked around, confused. "Where's the ring?"

Mickey gestured at the wreckage around them.

"Right here. Canvas is wherever you bleed on it."

Tyrell shook his head. "Man, you serious? We training next to a 1980s Buick?"

"Buick's got character," Mickey said. "Don't knock it."

He tossed Tyrell a pair of worn hand wraps.

"Wrap up. We're starting with tire drills."

Tyrell eyed the hill of bald rubber tires behind him.

"You mean like the ones behind every Planet Fitness dumpster?"

Mickey kicked a tire toward him.

"Flip it."

"Flip it?"

"Yeah. With your hands, genius."

Tyrell strained, flipped the tire once, nearly losing his balance. Mickey watched with the unimpressed patience of a man who'd seen every excuse in the book.

"Congratulations," Mickey said. "You just moved five inches of rubber. Only another forty yards to go."

"You trying to kill me or train me?"

"A little of both."

Tyrell couldn't help a smirk.

"You always this fun in the morning?"

He flipped the tire again—this time with a grunt. A real laugh escaped him, unexpected and bright in the cold air.

"You're nuts," he said.

"Takes one to train one," Mickey answered.

He pointed toward an engine block suspended from a crane chain.

"See that? You're gonna push it till I say stop."

Tyrell blinked. "That's an engine."

"Now you're catching on."

Tyrell put his hands on the cold steel and began to push. His breath fogged with each shove.

"You slow down," Mickey said, sipping his coffee, "I start singing."

Tyrell groaned. "Please don't."

"That's motivation right there."

Tyrell laughed again—the kind of laugh that meant something was finally cracking open.

Mickey caught himself smiling. Just a little.

* * *

The heater wheezed like it was dying. Mickey drove with both hands on the wheel, eyes forward, the way men drive when they've lived long enough to see everything go wrong at least once.

Tyrell slumped in the passenger seat, hoodie soaked with sweat, head lolling back.

He tapped the radio. Static.

Tapped again. More static.

"Yo," Tyrell said. "What decade is this radio from?"

"Same decade your footwork's stuck in," Mickey replied.

Tyrell laughed. "Relax. I'm trying to put on some music."

Mickey twisted the dial until a fuzzy station crackled through—1970s classic rock, distorted but recognizable.

"What even is this?" Tyrell muttered.

"That's Boston," Mickey said. "'More Than a Feeling.' Greatest intro ever recorded."

"This that old-people-at-cookouts music?"

"This is fighting music," Mickey said. "Came outta garages and union halls. Not whatever spaceship noise you listen to."

"Spaceship—?" Tyrell shook his head, grinning. "You wild. Lemme put my playlist on."

He reached for an AUX cord. Mickey slapped his hand away.

"Absolutely not."

"You ain't even heard it!"

"I already lived through the collapse of civilization once," Mickey said. "I'm not doing it again."

"Okay, grandpa. What you got against my generation?"

"Rhythm with no soul. Beats with no blood in 'em."

"You ever hear Kendrick?" Tyrell asked.

"No. And I don't want to."

"Man, he'd wreck half the dudes you used to walk out to."

"If he can throw a left hook, I'll reconsider."

Tyrell burst out laughing.

"Alright, old man. One song. If you hate it, I'll never touch the radio again."

Mickey sighed like this was physical suffering. "Fine. One."

Tyrell hooked up his cracked phone. The first beat dropped—deep, modern, with a pulse that shook the car.

Mickey flinched. "Jesus Christ. Turn it down."

"Nah, wait—listen to the lyrics," Tyrell said. "He talking about fighting himself. About pressure—"

Mickey listened. Against his will.

And slowly, grudgingly...

"...It's not the worst thing I ever heard," he muttered.

Tyrell grinned. "That's called growth, old man."

Mickey didn't deny it.

They drove on—two generations in one beat-up car, meeting in the middle without realizing it.

* * *

Chopper's office looked like a tornado made of canvas and sweat had blown through. Old hand wraps, fight posters, dusty trophies.

Tyrell stopped in the doorway.

"Chop… what was Mickey like? Back then."

Chopper didn't look up right away. He kept folding.

"Which part?" he said. "The parts people cheered for? Or the parts only I saw?"

Tyrell stepped in.

"The real part."

Chopper leaned back in his chair, thoughtful in a way that made the room feel smaller.

"Mickey was… a storm," he said. "You ever stand close to a storm, kid?"

Tyrell shook his head.

"Loud. Beautiful. Dangerous," Chopper said. "Left a mess every time—but damn if you didn't want to watch it roll in."

Tyrell took that in slowly.

"And he never believed he was good enough," Chopper said. "Even with belts on the wall. Even when crowds screamed his name. He had a hole in him nobody could fill."

Tyrell's jaw tightened. "He talks like he's got nothing left."

Chopper shook his head.

"Mick always talked like that. Even when he was twenty-two and bulletproof. The trick was… he kept showing up anyway."

Tyrell nodded, something settling in his chest.

"You think he's showing up for me?" he asked.

Chopper gave him a long, honest look.

"He's showing up because he's running out of chances," he said. "Don't waste the one he's giving you."

Tyrell swallowed.

Chopper pointed a finger. "Now get outta my office before I start telling you he used to cry watching sitcoms."

Tyrell barked out a laugh.

"You're full of shit."

"Yeah," Chopper said. "And so was he. That's why you two get along."

8

I'd Really Love to See You Tonight

The sky over Boston had gone gray by the time Mickey hit Dorchester Avenue, streetlights flickering to life ahead of schedule.

The radio buzzed softly through the static, then settled into an old song.

I'd really love to see you tonight...

Easy melody. Soft harmonies. The kind of thing he hadn't heard in years.

At first he didn't react. Just drove—past corner stores he used to duck into, bars that used to carry his fights on the small TVs behind the counter. Then the chorus came again, gentle and sad. And something in his chest shifted.

He wasn't sure whom he thought of first.

His father.

Maria.

Danny.

All of them, maybe.

"I'm not talking about moving in, and I don't want to change your life..."

Mickey's lips moved with the melody, though he wasn't sure of the words anymore. He remembered hearing it back in the late seventies, when he was young and hungry, bouncing from gym to gym, climbing the ladder. He'd drive with the windows down and swear the song was about the girl he'd call when he got home, about the future that felt wide open.

Now, sitting in the driver's seat many years later, the words felt slippery. Was it about a woman? A love that never quite fit? A longing for someone who was gone?

He didn't know. He only knew that the song made him ache.

His thoughts drifted to Danny—always to Danny. The boy he'd left behind too many times. The son who had learned to live without him. Mickey wondered if Danny ever thought about him when songs came on the radio, or if he'd tuned him out the way you tune out a bad station.

"I'd really love to see you tonight…"

The line repeated, and Mickey gripped the steering wheel tighter. He didn't know whom the voice was talking to, but in that moment, it might as well have been everyone he'd ever failed.

The rabbit foot swung from the dash, casting its crooked shadow across the windshield. A reminder of his bloodline, of how little luck Brannigan's ever had.

Mickey drove on through the night, the song crackling into silence, leaving him with nothing but the road ahead and the ghosts he carried in the back seat.

He kept driving, eyes on the road, but suddenly the city looked different— softer around the edges. A lump formed in his throat, the kind that felt like a punch that never landed but still stole your breath.

He reached up, turned the volume down—not off—and let the rest of the song bleed into the silence.

Funny, he thought. Of all the things that could break him… it was a love song on a Monday afternoon.

* * *

The faculty parking lot behind Arlington High School was nearly empty when Mickey pulled in. He killed the engine and just sat there. The late-afternoon sun made everything glow gold, but Mickey felt none of it. His stomach churned. Not from the cancer—this was something deeper. Something old. Something familiar.

The hallway smelled like pencil shavings. Teachers passed in pairs, exchanging weekend plans. Mickey walked through them like a ghost from another era.

He reached the open door of Room 218. Inside, Danny stood at the whiteboard, erasing the last of his lesson. Still dressed in slacks and rolled-up sleeves, his back was to the door.

Twenty feet back stood Mickey Brannigan.

Older now, his frame smaller than Danny remembered, his face pale and hollowed by illness. His bomber jacket looked too big for him, like the man inside had shrunk while the shell stayed the same. Students drifted between them, their chatter fading into white noise, like ghosts moving through a world that suddenly belonged only to the two of them. Neither man moved.

Danny's voice cut the air. "After all this time you have the balls to show up here?"

Mickey's throat worked before the words came. "Can we talk?"

"We're talking."

"I mean really talk," Mickey said quietly. "Five minutes. That's all I'm asking."

Danny's jaw flexed. "What do you want, Mick?"

"I just want a chance to talk with you."

"You don't need to explain anything. You made yourself perfectly clear... for most of my life."

Mickey swallowed. His voice carried the gravel of regret. "I was wrong. About everything."

"So what do you want?" Danny pressed.

"I wanted to see you."

Danny's eyes burned. "You weren't even at Mom's funeral."

Mickey's shoulders dipped as if the words themselves weighed him down. "I couldn't walk in there knowing what I'd done to her."

"She waited for you, you know," Danny shot back, voice trembling. "She always thought maybe—just maybe—you could change."

"Danny—"

"You left her alone. You left me alone."

Mickey closed his eyes for a beat, nodding slowly. "I know. And I'll carry that. Every day. I'm not asking you to forgive me. I just... I wanted to see your face again. I wanted to say I was sorry while I still had the breath to say it."

A long silence stretched between them. Danny didn't move, didn't blink. His voice cracked when the words came out. "You think I didn't need you? You were my hero when I was five. By ten, I was making up stories about where you were. By thirteen... I stopped talking about you at all."

Mickey's eyes glistened. "I know I don't deserve to be a part of your life. But I want to be. Even just a sliver."

"You don't get to choose now," Danny snapped.

"You're right," Mickey said, voice low. "My dad left too, but he didn't have a choice. I failed you, Danny. And I need to live with that."

"Then live with it," Danny said coldly, "and stay the hell out of my life."

"I'll go," Mickey murmured.

He turned, began walking toward . His voice wavered when he spoke again. "You have a son. I saw him once. Just for a moment. He looked happy. Like a kid who's gonna grow up knowing who he is. You did that."

Danny stayed silent.

Mickey nodded and started forward again.

"Mick."

The word slipped out before Danny could stop it. Mickey turned slightly, hope flickering in his tired eyes.

"You ever think," Danny said, voice raw, "that the bravest thing you could've done was just stay?"

Mickey's lips parted. "I just wanted one more round with you."

Danny's reply landed like a bell at the end of a fight. "We're all out of rounds."

They stood locked in silence, father and son, the distance between them measured in years of wounds. Mickey held Danny's gaze for one last moment, said nothing, then turned and walked away. It wasn't forgiveness. It wasn't even closure. It was something heavier.

Mickey walked in silence. Danny's voice still echoed in his head, each word a body shot he couldn't shake.

We're all out of rounds.

* * *

His fingers tightened around the steering wheel. The rejection stung deeper than he wanted to admit. Maybe he had destroyed the last chance to make amends for everything he had broken. But Mickey Brannigan had never been the kind of man who knew how to sit still. He needed to move, even when it hurt. Especially when it hurt.

So he went back to the only place that ever felt like home. The gym.

Inside, the air was alive with sound: fists on leather, ropes snapping against the floor, breath whistling through clenched teeth. Tyrell was there, sweat pouring, his gloves up, chest heaving as Mickey circled him like a wolf.

"Again!" Mickey barked. "Back on that bag! Feet sharp, hands tighter!"

Tyrell blinked, groaning. "We just ran six rounds, man."

"Don't talk. Punch."

Tyrell sucked in air, stepped to the heavy bag, and unleashed another flurry. The bag rocked back hard on its chain. Mickey stood with arms crossed, jaw tight. He wasn't saying much—but when he did, it cut like a jab.

"Keep your damn chin down, Ty. You want that pretty face rearranged?"

Tyrell stopped, turned. "What the hell is up with you today?"

"Punch."

Anger and confusion burned together in Tyrell's chest. He hit the bag again, harder this time.

Mickey stepped closer, voice like gravel. "Work is half of it. But discipline— that's the rest. You lose your head, you lose everything."

Tyrell let his gloves fall against his thighs. "Why you coming at me like this? This ain't about me. You're mad at somebody else."

For a moment, Mickey's mask slipped. His eyes softened. "I saw my son today."

Tyrell's shoulders sank. "Didn't go well?"

Mickey shook his head, sharp and short. "He looked right through me. Like I was already a ghost."

Tyrell sat on the edge of the ring, peeled one glove off with his teeth. "You think yelling at me is gonna fix that?"

Mickey didn't reply.

"You want me ready for my first pro fight?" Tyrell asked, locking eyes with him. "Then train me. Push me, fine. But don't punish me because of your past."

Mickey looked away, shame written in the lines of his face. Tyrell tossed both gloves aside and grabbed a towel.

"Look—I'm not him," Tyrell said. "And I'm not trying to be."

Mickey sighed. "I know."

"But I'm here," Tyrell pressed. "You want to build me into something great? Cool. But don't break me in the process."

The words landed heavier than any punch Mickey had taken.

Hands up," Mickey barked. "You walk into a gym, you're already fighting. Don't ever drop your guard."

Tyrell scrambled to raise his fists. They felt heavy, awkward. Mickey stood, adjusted Tyrell's elbows with surprising gentleness, then smacked his gloves back into place.

"Again. Chin down. You're showing me the whole street—tuck it."

For the next hour, Tyrell's world shrank to the rhythm of Mickey's voice: step, pivot, jab—again. Every correction was sharp, but every nod felt like winning a championship. By the time his arms ached and sweat poured down his back, he realized somebody believed he could do this.

As he peeled the gloves off, Mickey clapped a heavy hand on his shoulder.

Tyrell tried not to smile, but the warmth in his chest was impossible to hide.

Mickey leaned back against the ropes, wiping his brow with the edge of a towel. He'd been in gyms his whole damn life, seen a hundred kids come and go—most of them soft, some of them mean, a few who had the right mix of both. But there was something different in the Banks kid.

Tyrell wasn't just swinging his fists. He was fighting ghosts. Fighting the kids who pushed him in school halls, the men who disappeared on him, the weight of a world that told him he'd never make it out. Mickey recognized that look—it was the same one he'd had at seventeen when all he wanted was a way out of Southie.

And for the first time in years, Mickey felt that old spark. The excitement of shaping someone. Of passing on what he knew, the little tricks that only a lifetime in the ring could teach—how to breathe through pain, how to use silence to rattle an opponent, how to stay on your feet when everything inside you screamed to fall.

But the spark carried a shadow. His body wasn't what it used to be. The doctors hadn't given him a clock, but Mickey felt it ticking every morning when he woke up.

He's got it, Mickey thought. *He's got what you can't teach. But do I have enough time to give him the rest?*

9

My Girl

Morning began at 5:02 a.m., the kind of hour where most of the city was still dreaming. Tyrell was not. He ran through the cold streets with his hood up, breath turning white in the dawn air, shoes slapping the pavement in a rhythm he hoped would one day mean something.

By mid-morning the gym was awake—if a place like Chopper's could ever really sleep. Mickey swept the floor with one hand, slow and methodical, while Tyrell jumped rope with the intensity of someone racing his own doubt. Sweat hit the mats in steady drops. Mickey paused the broom long enough to tap Tyrell's ankle with the handle, shifting his foot an inch. No lecture, no speech. Just correction.

In the afternoon Tyrell went to war with the heavy bag. His fists worked in vicious loops, each punch aimed at some invisible ghost. His knuckles burned beneath the wraps, skin rubbed raw, but he didn't stop. Pain wasn't the enemy—it was proof he was trying.

Night brought the ice bath. Tyrell sat in a metal tub behind the gym, a cloud of steam rising off him as the last light folded behind the buildings. Mickey handed him a towel and a protein shake the way a parent might hand a kid a jacket—silent, necessary, unspoken care.

The next morning, Chopper watched from the office window. He didn't call out or comment. He just stood there, hands on his hips, head tilted slightly. A faint smile tugged at the corner of his mouth—the kind he wouldn't admit

59

to.

By the end of the week, Tyrell was shadowboxing under a lone ring light, skin gleaming with sweat, every movement sharp, controlled. Mickey stayed back in the darkened corner, arms folded, eyes shining with something he tried to blink away—pride, exhaustion, maybe both.

Tyrell finished a final combination and turned toward him.

No speech. No swagger. Just a nod.

Mickey nodded back.

Two men who didn't need words to understand each other.

* * *

Mickey and Tyrell shared a booth, two cheeseburgers vanishing between them, fries scattered like confetti, and two sweating chocolate milkshakes standing guard.

Tyrell talked with his hands, his voice animated.

"You should've seen her, man," he said, laughing. "This chick at the bagel spot—skin like brown sugar, attitude like she owned the whole block. I gave her one look, and boom—number in my phone before I even finished my cinnamon raisin."

Mickey grinned. "You ever stop to wonder if she gave you that number just to get you to shut up?"

"Oh come on," Tyrell said. "Look at me. Six foot, handsome, undefeated in the amateurs."

"You sure don't lack confidence."

"You ever run game back in the day?" Tyrell asked. "Bet girls were climbing over ropes for you."

Mickey wiped his mouth with a napkin. "There were a few. But only one that really mattered."

Tyrell paused, taken by the change in Mickey's tone.

"So who was the one?"

"Maria," Mickey said softly. "She was everything."

"What was she like?"

Mickey's face warmed at the memory.

"Sharp. Beautiful like she didn't know it. She had this laugh… like it came from someplace holy."

Tyrell leaned back. "I ain't never loved anyone like that."

"One day you might," Mickey said. "And when it happens, you'll know right away. Just make sure you don't push her away chasing something that'll never love you back."

Silence settled over the booth. The waitress dropped the check off with a smile. Mickey grabbed it.

"I got it," Tyrell said.

"You'll get the next one," Mickey replied. "After your first pro win. Tonight's on me."

Tyrell smirked. "I'll hold you to that."

He watched Mickey for a moment, something thoughtful in his eyes.

"You ever think she'd be proud of you now?" he asked.

"Nah," he said. "But maybe… she'd smile seeing me try."

Tyrell nodded, letting the moment breathe.

Mickey cleared his throat. "You want to go sightseeing?"

* * *

The suburban station looked forgotten by time. Chain-link fences rattled in the cold wind. The tracks lay dark and empty, waiting for a train that felt like it might never come.

Mickey and Tyrell sat on a bench, shoulders hunched, warm breath drifting into the chilled air.

"This where you come to think?" Tyrell asked, scanning the empty platform. "Looks dead out here."

"That's the point," Mickey said, eyes fixed on the tracks. "Peace don't always look pretty, kid. Sometimes it's just quiet."

Tyrell leaned forward, elbows on knees. "Why here though? A train station?"

Mickey took a long breath, his voice softening as memory washed over him.

"Long time ago," he said. "I brought Maria to a Celtics game. We got off at the wrong stop—middle of nowhere, twenty degrees, no cabs. Only thing we could do was walk."

Tyrell listened, unusually still.

"I wrapped her inside my coat," Mickey said. "Held her close the whole way. She was freezing, but laughing. Told me I smelled like peanuts and cheap cologne."

A faint grin tugged at his mouth.

"That walk… that was one of the happiest nights of my life."

Tyrell nodded slowly.

"So the champ's best memory… is walking to the next stop in the cold."

"That's what people don't get," Mickey said. "It ain't the fights. It's the moments in between."

A distant rumble grew across the tracks.

A train burst past them, lights flashing over their faces, wind roaring through the empty platform. Neither moved. They just watched it.

"She wouldn't want you sad," Tyrell said quietly.

"I ain't sad," Mickey replied. "Just… sometimes you realize the best parts went quicker than you thought."

The train vanished into the dark.

Tyrell looked at Mickey—really looked at him—and something wordless passed between them.

Something like understanding.

10

History at the Door

The fight gym was alive with sound. Tyrell worked the mitts with one of the younger trainers, his jab snapping like a whip, his footwork light and sure. He was locked in, focused, until the gym door creaked open.

A shady figure entered.

Carmine Russo.

He looked like a relic from another age that refused to be buried. A long leather coat swayed at his knees. Gold rings glittered on three fingers. His gray hair was slicked back, nightclub—smooth, as if he were about to step onstage with a microphone instead of into a gym. His smile came easy—too easy—the kind of grin that never meant anything good.

Tyrell didn't notice him at first. But Chopper did. From the window of the office upstairs, the old trainer's jaw tightened, the look of a man who'd just swallowed something sour.

Carmine walked through the gym like he owned it. Like his name still meant something. Maybe it did, in the crooked corners of the city where men like him never truly disappeared. He stopped to watch Tyrell move—fast, powerful, sharp angles, combinations that cracked against the mitts with promise.

Carmine clapped once, slow. "Jesus," he muttered. "That kid's got something."

Tyrell turned. The trainer froze, mitts down.

"You with the press?" Tyrell asked.

Carmine chuckled. "Nah. I'm a friend." He held out a hand.

"Tyrell Banks, yeah?" the man said, voice smooth as a sales pitch.

Tyrell kept his hands up a second longer, breath tapering. "That's me."

"Name's Carmine Russo. You don't know me yet, but you will."

From the corner, Mickey pushed off the locker, the old metal groaning at his shoulder. "You don't need to know him."

Carmine's grin widened, teeth flashing. "Easy, Brick. I'm just introducing myself to the future of the middleweight division."

"You mean the latest name you can slap on a T-shirt before bleeding him dry," Mickey said.

Carmine turned his attention back to the kid, as if Mickey were a creak in the floor. "Your coach is cute when he's pissed," he told Tyrell. "But I'm here to talk business."

Tyrell let his hands fall, the wraps damp and tight against his wrists. "What kind of business?"

"Sponsorship. Social media contracts. A path to the big-time. You like Vegas? Like crowds chanting your name? I get you there. No more small-time showcases in busted gyms with squeaky floorboards."

Mickey stood up straight, the temperature in his voice dropping ten degrees. "Get out."

Carmine's smirk didn't budge. "Still mad about the Corte fight? You begged for that card slot."

"You booked me as a stepping stone," Mickey said. "You knew I was done and you fed me to a killer."

"I didn't make you climb in the ring," Carmine said, shrugging. "You just didn't know when to quit."

"I quit," Mickey said quietly, "the day I stopped listening to myself."

Carmine tipped his chin at Tyrell. "You really want to end up like him? Broke. Broken. Sleeping in a supply closet full of jock straps and mildew?"

Tyrell's jaw tightened. "He was a great fighter."

"That doesn't translate to money, kid." Carmine stepped closer, lowering his voice like he was letting Tyrell in on a secret. "I've worked with champs.

You got hands, you got a look, and you got a window that's closing every second you waste in this glorified antique shop."

Mickey didn't move. His eyes never left Tyrell. "If you go with him, you'll make money," he said, voice low. "Fast. But you'll wake up five years from now wondering who the hell you are. If you stay here, you'll earn every inch. And you'll still be you when it's over."

Tyrell looked from Carmine to Mickey, breathing through his nose. For a heartbeat, temptation flashed—bright and obvious—then it flickered out.

"I'm good where I am," Tyrell said.

For a second, Carmine's face hardened, something mean showing through the polish. Then the smile came back. "Your funeral, kid." He turned toward the door. "If you wise up, I'm one call away."

The door banged shut, leaving the gym in its usual hum—bags swaying, lights buzzing, the old building settling in its bones. Tyrell and Mickey met eyes. No smiles. Just a nod that meant more than both of them would say.

A few minutes later, Tyrell sat on the ring apron. Mickey leaned on the ropes, the adrenaline bleeding out of him, the ache returning to his joints like bad weather.

"That guy always that greasy?" Tyrell asked.

"That guy's why half the fighters from my era are bartenders with blown out knees and unpaid medical bills," Mickey said.

"He wasn't wrong about Vegas, though."

"We'll get you there," Mickey said. "The right way. No shortcuts. No vultures."

"Good," Tyrell said. He flicked a strip of tape onto the mat. "'Cause I'm not trying to be a product. I'm trying to be a problem."

Mickey laughed—the first clean sound he'd made in days. "Carmine's a taker," he said after a moment. "He empties you out, then walks away."

"I thought Chopper set up your fights," Tyrell said.

"Chopper trained me." Mickey's voice softened on the name. "But Carmine booked the fights."

"So you guys got history."

"In '89 I lost the title," Mickey said. "Held it three years. You wake up one morning and everything feels different."

"But you still made bank, right?"

"Not really. Carmine took his cut and I blew the rest."

"You never got it back?"

"Heck no." Mickey shook his head. "I got moved down to the mid-card. Became a stepping stone for fighters like you."

Tyrell nodded slowly. "So we don't need him."

"There's a dozen Carmine Russo running the streets," Mickey said. "But what you got—speed, skill, fire—you can't teach that. He needs you. You don't need him."

He reached out and set his hand on Tyrell's shoulder. It was nothing dramatic—just weight and warmth, steady and sure. For Mickey, it was the first real gesture of connection he'd allowed in a long time. Tyrell didn't pull away.

Mickey memories dragged him back.

He remembered the slow decline: still a draw in the early '90s, still enough to get his name in bold on the posters. But the truth was clear—he was the test, the stepping stone for someone else's rise. Frankie Torres in '93. Rafe Alvarez in '94. They were younger, hungrier, faster. They got the headlines. Carmine got his cut. Mickey got the bruises.

By 2001 the calls had slowed. The casinos stopped booking him. The TV slots dried up.

So he went where the calls still came: VFW halls, high school gyms, old hotel ballrooms with rings that wobbled and announcers who mispronounced his name. He fought men with losing records, journeymen clawing for gas money. The crowds were thin, the purses thinner. Still, he told himself it was temporary. That the next call would be the one.

Mickey remembered a night years back, holed up in Atlantic City between fights. Not the Four Seasons, not the Ritz like when he was riding high, but a Best Western with threadbare carpet and a buzzing neon sign outside the window that never shut off.

He sat on the edge of the bed, staring out at the strip below. Directly across the street stood a church, the kind where parishioners filed in on Sunday mornings with pressed shirts and solemn faces. And right beside it—a sex shop with blacked-out windows and a sign that flashed ADULT XXX in red.

Mickey chuckled to himself at the time. "Never seen God's house and the Devil's playground sharing a parking lot," he muttered, shaking his head. "Atlantic City—hell of a place."

He thought about how things used to be. Back when he was champ, the promoters comped him suites at the Four Seasons, room service trays with silver lids, silk robes draped over the chair. Now the mattress sagged in the middle, and the shower handle came off in his hand when he turned it too far.

He lay back on the stiff sheets and laughed at the absurdity of it all—the church bells on Sunday clashing with the hum of neon from next door, the sound of salvation and sin bleeding into each other.

"Guess that's me," Mickey whispered. "Half preacher, half sinner. Stuck somewhere in between."

It was the kind of moment that told him life had a way of humbling you, whether you wanted it or not.

Later that same night, restless in the Best Western, Mickey decided to take a walk. The boardwalk was mostly empty, save for drunks leaning against railings and hustlers looking for their next mark. Atlantic City always had a way of showing you its teeth after midnight.

He walked with his hands shoved in his jacket pockets, collar up against the sea wind, passing shuttered pizza shops and the glow of a twenty-four-hour liquor store.

Out of nowhere, a voice barked:

"Hey, you! You're a bum!"

Mickey turned. Standing there under a flickering streetlight was a little man—barely came up to his chest—pointing a stubby finger at him. His face was red from drink, his grin wild, but his words were sharp as a jab.

"You hear me? Bum!" the man laughed, rocking on his heels.

For a moment Mickey thought about firing back, about telling the guy who he was—former champ, fought under the lights, stayed at the Four Seasons when men like you couldn't even get through the door. But the words stuck in his throat. Because looking down at his scuffed boots and the cheap Best Western key card in his pocket, Mickey realized the little guy wasn't entirely wrong.

The final insult came years later, in a half-empty VFW hall in Fall River. Cigarette smoke hung low over the lights. Mickey's name was called—but not even right.

"Mickey Branham."

No one bothered to correct it.

11

Secrets

The front door creaked open like it was sighing. Angela stepped inside, shoulders slumped, her scrubs wrinkled from a twelve-hour shift that looked like it had taken twelve years off her life. She set her purse down and rubbed her temples as if they hurt in a way sleep couldn't fix.

"You still up?" she asked.

Tyrell shrugged, half joking, half weary.

"Somebody's gotta feed them."

Angela glanced at the stove, then at the kids—Malik hunched over his bowl, Kiesha chewing like she hadn't eaten in a day. Something in her face softened, then hardened again just as quickly. She pulled out a chair and sat.

"Smells like you didn't burn it this time," she murmured.

"Progress," Tyrell said, handing out bowls of mac and cheese like it was a holiday feast. The kids attacked the food instantly. Angela made herself a plate and ate slower, more deliberate, the exhaustion still humming in her bones.

"You working tomorrow?" she asked.

"Training."

Angela set her fork down with a heavy clink.

"Training ain't work."

"It's work if I'm trying to make something of it."

Her voice sharpened, rising like a whip.

"Make something of it? Tyrell, I'm busting my ass at that hospital so you don't have to live the same life."

"You don't get it," he snapped. "It's different."

"What's so different about it? I don't see you getting paid."

The kids froze—the kind of stillness children learn early when storms hit their house.

Tyrell leaned against the counter, jaw tight enough to crack.

"So what?" he shot back. "You want me bagging groceries? Sweeping floors? That your plan for me?"

"It's called responsibility," she said. "You need to start somewhere."

Tyrell slammed the spoon into the sink; metal rang out sharp and final.

"I'm not giving up just 'cause life's hard!"

Angela shot to her feet, fury blazing through the exhaustion.

"You think I gave up?"

Her voice shook the room.

"Don't you dare," she said, chest rising. "Everything I've done was so you kids didn't go hungry. So you had a shot at something better. And all I see is you wasting it—chasing some pipe dream that's gonna leave you broken like every other fool who thought he was special."

Tyrell's voice cracked open, raw and loud—

"I am special!"

The words echoed off the walls...and off his own fear.

His breath shuddered.

"I have to be," he whispered. "It's all I got."

Angela's eyes glistened. She swallowed the tears, refusing to let them fall.

"Baby… you're not the only one I worry about. Malik. Kiesha. They need you too."

Tyrell jerked his chair back, the legs scraping the floor in a violent protest.

"I fight so you don't have to," he said.

He grabbed his hoodie.

Malik stood. "Ty—"

Kiesha's voice cracked. "Don't go…"

Tyrell hesitated—guilt flickering like a faulty bulb—but he couldn't stay.

He pulled the hoodie on, head down, and walked out.

* * *

A gray sky pressed low over the cemetery, wind cutting through the bare branches like something searching for a place to land. Mickey trudged up the narrow path with a white rose clenched in his hand.

He stopped at a modest stone:
MARIA BRANNIGAN — 1958–2007
Beloved Wife and Mother.

He stood there, breathing hard, fighting the cold and everything else.
Finally he dropped to his knees; the gravel crunched beneath him.
"Hey, Mare..." he whispered.
"I never listened to a word, did I?"
The wind whipped across his face. He wiped his mouth, blinked hard.
"You always were the brave one," he said.
The confession broke him.
His breath hitched; his shoulders shook. Tears came hot and fast.
"I been calling myself a fighter my whole damn life," he choked out.
He leaned forward until his forehead touched the cold stone. The last bit of pride he had left cracked.
"I ran from Danny. From you."
His voice splintered.
"And now there's nothing left to run from."
The sobs came messy, unfiltered—the kind a man hides for decades until they tear out of him. The wind swallowed the sound, carrying pieces of him across the bare field.
"You stayed when it hurt," he whispered.
His fist slammed the frozen ground—then he cradled the hand like a child. He stayed there, broken open, alone in the cold.
After a long moment, he set the rose gently at the base of the stone. His

fingers lingered.

"You were the wings, Mare," he said softly. "Always were."

He bowed his head and cried.

* * *

The gym sat in darkness except for a single flickering EXIT sign. Tyrell slipped inside, hoodie soaked, eyes red with anger. He kicked a stray glove; it skidded under a bench.

He walked past the ring—silent now—toward the back hallway.

One door was ajar.

He hesitated, then knocked lightly.

No answer.

He pushed it open.

The room was small, almost monastic—a cot, a desk, a humming space heater.

A brown paper bag sat open on the desk. Beside it lay a bottle of pills: ***PANCRELIPASE — TAKE WITH FOOD.***

Tyrell stared. Slowly the truth dawned, heavy and suffocating.

"...shit," he whispered.

He picked up the bottle, turned it in his hand, then set it down gently, as though rough handling might make reality worse.

On the mirror was a taped photograph—Mickey in his prime, gloves raised, grinning beside a woman and a small boy.

Tyrell stepped closer. He touched the edge of the photo with a thumb, tracing the kid's smile.

He sat on the edge of Mickey's bed and exhaled—a long, defeated breath.

A moment later he lay back—not meaning to sleep, just meaning to stop thinking.

The gym creaked around him like an old house sharing a secret.

Tyrell closed his eyes.

For the first time in a long while, he didn't feel alone.

12

In Case You Never Hear It

He'd dug it out earlier that day from the back of the closet, still in its cracked leather case, dust clinging to it like a memory no one wanted.

A message.

For Danny.

Mickey turned the camcorder over in his hands, feeling the weight of it. What would he even say?

Hey, son, it's me. Your old man. I'm sorry I missed your childhood because I was too busy trying to feel important.

No. Too pathetic.

Danny, I should've been better. I should've shown you how to be a man without bleeding for it.

Closer. But still not right.

He pictured his son's face, the last time they'd stood in front of each other. Danny's eyes had been stone. That wall between them wasn't just made of years—it was built of Mickey's choices. And mortar like that doesn't break easy.

He stared at his own reflection in the tiny screen. Gray hair. Weathered skin. Eyes hollowed out by illness and regret. Not the man Danny remembered. Maybe not even the man Danny hated.

Mickey pressed record. The red light blinked. He sat frozen for a long moment before his throat gave way.

"Danny," he began, voice low. "If you're watching this, it means I didn't get to tell you in person. Maybe that's my fault. Hell, it's probably all my fault. But I want you to know something… I was proud of you. Even when I didn't say it. Even when I didn't act like it. Especially then."

He stopped. The silence pressed back against him, heavier than the blinking light.

"I didn't want you to be me, kid. I wanted you to be better. I still do. That's the whole point of this. If I can give you anything—anything at all—it's the mistakes I made, so you don't have to repeat 'em."

The locker room door creaked. Tyrell emerged with a towel slung around his neck. He froze when he saw Mickey hunched at the table, camcorder blinking.

"What are you doing?" Tyrell asked.

Mickey didn't answer at first. Finally, he looked up, voice gravelly. "I was thinking of filming something."

"Like… a video?"

Mickey nodded. "For Danny. In case I don't get the chance. I want him to know some things. That I'm sorry. That I loved him. That I was never as strong outside the ring as I tried to be in it. I thought maybe if he heard it in my voice, he'd believe it more."

Tyrell sat down on the bench across from him. His voice was quiet, but steady. "Nah. That's not it."

Mickey frowned. "What do you mean?"

"I mean that's not how this ends, Mick. You don't get to wrap it up in a neat little bow. Not with a video."

"I don't know if I'll get the opportunity."

"Then make the opportunity." Tyrell's tone was firm, but without edge. "Look, I never knew my dad. Not really. He split when I was born. Left my mom raising us in a two-bedroom with roaches in the toaster and water leaking through the ceiling. He never came back. Never called. And yeah, I hated him. Still kinda do."

Mickey's eyes flickered, unreadable.

"But if that man ever showed up at my door, face to face, and said 'I'm sorry'—you know what I'd want?" Tyrell leaned forward. "I'd want him to say it looking me in the eye. So I could know it was real. So I could feel it. You don't say goodbye to your son through a damn camera. You look him in the eyes. All of it. The truth."

Mickey swallowed hard. "I don't know if he'll even talk to me."

"Doesn't matter," Tyrell said. "It's not about whether he forgives you. It's about whether you're finally man enough to show up."

Silence stretched between them until Mickey slowly powered off the camcorder. He let it sit, dead weight, on the table. "You think he'll listen?"

Tyrell stood, clapped him lightly on the shoulder. "I don't know. But I know you'll never forgive yourself if you don't try."

For the first time in days, a spark flickered in Mickey's chest. Hope—but fragile. Then the pain returned, hot in his stomach, making him grip the table until it passed. Not day by day now. Minute by minute.

Time wasn't on his side.

* * *

The next morning, Mickey sat on the crinkled paper of the exam table. Shirt off. Body mapped in scars. A museum of pain, each mark a relic of nights when he refused to fall.

The physician assistant entered briskly. Late twenties. Clipboard clutched like armor. Her badge read S. Hathaway, PA-C. She didn't look at him when she spoke.

"Michael Brannigan, age sixty-three. What are you here for?"

"I've got pain," Mickey said evenly. "Stomach mostly. Bathroom stuff too. I know what this is, doc."

"I'm not a doctor," she snapped. "Just a physician assistant. You were diagnosed with pancreatic adenocarcinoma six months ago. Declined chemotherapy?"

Mickey studied her like she was the sick one. No bedside. Just words like bullets.

"With the progression of your symptoms," she continued briskly, "it's likely the disease has advanced to the liver and bile ducts. Pale stools, jaundice, pain. Your prognosis is… not good."

He swallowed, not because he didn't know, but because hearing it laid out so cold stung worse than the tumor.

"You could have said that with a little grace," he murmured.

She looked up, startled. "I don't mean to be disrespectful—"

"But you are." He buttoned his shirt with slow, shaking hands. "I get it. You see fifty people a day complaining. I came in here knowing I'm dying—just looking for a little decency."

Something flickered in her expression, but no apology came. Mickey pulled on his jacket, tightening it around his shoulders.

"You got a long career ahead of you," he said quietly. "Maybe learn how to talk to people before this job turns you into a machine."

He left without another word.

* * *

The bar was called O'Malley's now, but the ghosts still knew it as Murphy's. Mickey spotted him down the bar. Patrick Jennings.

Back then, Patrick had been a middleweight everyone in Boston respected. Not the fastest. Not the flashiest. But the toughest. A fighter who could take a beating, eat every punch thrown his way, and keep moving forward. Mickey had sparred him a dozen times, and each round felt like trying to wear down a brick wall. Patrick never broke the top ten, but every man who laced gloves in Boston knew you had to kill him to stop him.

Now his shoulders had caved in on themselves. His right hand trembled as he raised a glass of Jameson, the years and the damage finally catching up to the toughest man Mickey had ever known.

Mickey slid onto the stool beside him. "You buying the next one?"

Patrick squinted, then grinned. "Well, I'll be damned. Brannigan. Thought you were dead."

"Not yet." Mickey raised a hand. "Two more."

They sat in the old fighter's silence—measuring what time had stolen.

"You still got it in the eyes," Patrick said finally. "Mean when you need to be. What are you doing now outside the ring?"

"Training a kid. Good one."

Patrick chuckled, dry. "I train kids too. Teach 'em to keep their hands up. To stay outta trouble. Don't want 'em ending up like me." He tapped his temple. "Parkinson's. Doctor says it's from the shots. Said I should've quit earlier."

"You were never the quitting type," Mickey said.

"Neither were you. That's the problem with us."

The bartender dropped the drinks. They clinked glasses.

"You remember Worcester?" Patrick asked, a smile tugging at his mouth. "Busted my nose in the second round. Kept going. You told me I was too dumb to quit."

"Yeah," Mickey said, grinning.

Patrick's smile faded. "Funny thing about regret. It ain't just the fights you lost. It's the people you hurt chasing the ones you wanted to win."

"Your boy?" Patrick asked.

Mickey's silence was answer enough.

Patrick nodded. "Time's the only thing you can't fight, Mick. But it's the only thing that can fix some things too."

Mickey drained his glass. "You sound like you should be the one in the corner, not me."

Patrick grinned, crooked tooth flashing. "Hell, Mick... I'm in everybody's corner now. Just don't wait until you're shaking like me to make things right."

They lingered there, trading old names, old stories, until the ice melted in their glasses.

13

Love Hurts

The late afternoon sun stretched long shadows across the sidewalk outside JP Licks in Lexington. The bell above the door jingled as Danny shouldered it open, Caleb bounding in behind him with the kind of endless energy only eleven-year-old's seemed to have.

"What are you getting?" Danny asked as they stepped up to the counter.

"Cookie dough," Caleb replied instantly. "And brownie batter. Together."

Danny raised an eyebrow. "That's… excessive."

"Mom never lets me do both."

Danny smirked. "Well, I'm not Mom, am I?"

Caleb grinned wide, all teeth. Danny paid, tipping the high school kid behind the register a little more than necessary, then carried their cones outside to one of the small wrought-iron tables on the sidewalk.

"You got plans this weekend?" Danny asked casually. "Maybe we could go to the park again. The one with the pond and the tennis courts?"

Caleb nodded through a mouthful of ice cream. "Yeah. That'd be good."

The air was cool. Cars hummed past, a dog barked somewhere down the street.

"Dad?" Caleb said suddenly, eyes on his cone. "Can I ask you something?"

Danny straightened. "Always."

"Were you close with your dad?"

The question hit him off guard. Not here. Not over ice cream. Danny hesitated, then said carefully, "Not really."

"Why not?"

Danny studied his son, thought about the easy answer, then pushed it aside. Caleb deserved more than that.

"He was… complicated," Danny said finally. "He was a boxer. A real one. Championship belt and everything. But he didn't always know how to be a dad. And I didn't always know how to forgive that."

Caleb frowned, processing. "So you stopped talking?"

"Yeah. For a long time."

Danny thought of Mickey's fists raised in those old black-and-white fight photos. Thought of being five years old, carried high on Mickey's shoulders after his championship victories, both of them screaming with joy. Then the birthdays missed. Maria crying in the kitchen. The silence that became a second language.

Caleb leaned back, satisfied. "I think you're a good dad."

Danny laughed despite himself. He reached out and ruffled Caleb's hair. "You're a good kid."

Caleb let it happen for a heartbeat, then pulled away in that boyish way that said too much affection wasn't cool. They sat in silence, watching people pass.

Later that night, after Caleb had fallen asleep sprawled across his bed with a hockey stick clutched in one hand, Danny stood at the kitchen window.

Danny didn't know why the memory came to him now. Maybe it was the way Caleb had looked at him. Maybe it was that question about whether people could change. Or maybe it was the ice cream—the simple joy of it, the closeness. A reminder of something he hadn't let himself feel in years.

He was six again. Moakley Park. A summer evening. Mickey had taken him there after a workout. Danny sat on the swings, the sky painted gold-orange, chains creaking as Mickey pushed gently with the heel of his boot.

"You know how much I love you?" Mickey had asked.

Danny giggled. "How much?"

Mickey spread his hands wide. "This much." Then wider still. "Nope. This much."

Finally he pulled his son into his arms, kneeling until they were eye-to-eye. "More than anything in this world. You got that, Danny-boy? More than anything."

Danny had nodded solemnly. "I'll always be there for you, Dad."

"And I'll always be there for you," Mickey had said. "No matter what."

Now, decades later, the words echoed like ghosts. Danny sipped from his glass of water, eyes fixed on the quiet street.

Where had that man gone? The man who knelt in the grass and said those words?

He thought of another memory.

The night Caleb was born. January, streets filled with dirty snow, headlights cutting across the wet pavement. He hadn't slept in two days. Pacing the waiting room one moment, gripping Lena's hand the next. And then, finally, Caleb James Brannigan—seven pounds, four ounces—his perfect little fist wrapped around Danny's finger.

The world had gone quiet. Except for the phone on the hospital wall. Danny had kept glancing at it, waiting. Hoping. For his father.

The call never came.

Not congratulations. Not even a message. Just silence.

Danny set the empty glass gently on the counter. He didn't cry. But something in him shifted. He wasn't sure what it meant yet. Only that the memory hadn't faded.

And maybe, that meant something.

***

Across the city, another man couldn't sleep.

Mickey Brannigan lurched from his mattress to the bathroom, gripping the sink like it might keep him standing. His stomach clenched, sharp and merciless. He barely made it to the toilet before he vomited. Bitter bile burned his throat. He coughed, spat, wiped his mouth with the back of his hand.

The mirror above the sink caught him when he finally lifted his head.

Gray stubble. Skin yellowed at the edges. Eyes sunk into shadowed hollows. He looked like a man already half-buried. His hands shook as he gripped the porcelain, knuckles pale.

He splashed cold water on his face, but it didn't wash away the truth. His body was failing.

When Mickey first heard the words, PANCREATIC CANCER, it was the silence afterward that cut deepest.

For a strange, fleeting moment, he almost smiled. Not out of courage, but out of something darker. Relief. Because maybe this meant he'd see Maria again. Maybe, finally, he could sit with her the way he did on that bench at the station—the wrong stop that had felt like the right place in the world.

But then the relief curdled. The thought came quick, sharp: *What if I don't make it to her? What if I don't deserve it?*

He shifted in the chair, his knuckles tightening on the jacket. Maria had been light, laughter, a kind of grace he never understood why she gave him. Mickey wasn't sure heaven had a spot for men who drank too much, fought too long, and turned their backs on their own family. And if by some miracle he did get through the gates, maybe Maria wouldn't even want to see him. Maybe she'd already let go.

The doctor kept talking—treatment options, clinical trials, timelines—but Mickey wasn't listening. His thoughts had gone elsewhere. To Danny.

Unfinished business. The two words pressed on his chest heavier than any diagnosis. He pictured his son's face, younger, watching from the gym steps like Chopper had reminded him. The way he used to look at Mickey.

"I need to… talk to him," Mickey muttered, more to himself than to the doctor. His voice cracked. "I need to fix it."

But even as he said it, fear crawled up his throat. Because what if Danny didn't want fixing? What if Mickey showed up, cancer eating him alive, and his son shut the door in his face? Worse yet—what if Danny opened it, and Mickey still didn't know what the hell to say?

The doctor's voice faded back in: "Mr. Brannigan, do you understand?"

Mickey nodded, though his mind was far away. He understood too much. Death was coming, and with it, the ghosts he'd tried to outrun—Maria, Danny, every fight he'd lost outside the ring.

His hands were shaking, because for the first time in his life, Mickey Brannigan was afraid not of dying—but of facing the people he loved on the other side.

14

Moment of Truth

Danny sat in his car outside Chopper's Gym. For weeks, maybe months, he'd rehearsed this night in his head. He pictured himself storming into the gym and finally spitting out the words that had lived in his throat for decades: You don't get to come back now. You don't get to decide when you're a father.

Danny gripped the wheel tighter. His hands shook. His stomach churned. He thought about turning the key and driving off, like he'd done before. But something about today felt different. Caleb's questions. The memory of Maria. The ache that never softened.

He shut off the engine and stepped into the cold night. The closer he got, the louder his pulse became, like a drum in his ears.

His hand hovered on the door handle.

Just open it. Walk in. Say it.

And then the door burst outward, slamming against the wall.

Danny flinched back.

Carmine Russo entered before Danny.

"Well, well," Carmine's voice drawled, oily and smooth. "If it ain't the Brannigan Revival Tour."

Danny froze, half in shadow, unseen. Carmine wasn't talking to him.

"I come in peace," Carmine went on, arms spreading wide in mock sincerity.

83

"Really. Brought someone I think your boy might wanna meet."

From behind him stepped a broad-shouldered figure. Seamus "The Bear" Doherty. Irish, thick through the chest and arms, his presence filled the doorway like a storm cloud. His eyes landed on Tyrell instantly. And they stayed there.

Carmine grinned. "Undefeated. Ten knockouts. Talk of the Dublin circuit. Just inked with Topline Sports. First American card in three weeks. We need someone to test his chin. Put your boy in with him—win or lose, he gets seen. ESPN cameras. HBO sniffing around. You want exposure? This is it."

Tyrell had been bouncing lightly in the ring, sweat glistening down his temples. But now he stilled, his eyes narrowing, fixed on Seamus.

The Irishman stepped forward, voice low and cold. "They say you've got speed," he said. "Let's see how fast you fall."

Tyrell's voice came back calm, almost detached. "I don't fall for hype."

Carmine clapped once, grinning wider. "Kid's got stones. I like it. But let me tell you something—the fight game don't hold elevators. You jump when the doors open."

That's when Mickey's voice cut in, rough as gravel. "Not this one. He's not your stepping stone."

The grin vanished from Carmine's face. His tone turned sharp. "You were a name once, Mick. I respected that. But this ain't your story anymore. You had your title. You had your time. Don't drag this kid into the shadows with you."

He flicked a gold-embossed card onto the apron. It landed face up, glinting under the gym lights.

"Sleep on it," Carmine said. "Just don't take too long."

He turned, gave Seamus a nod. The two swaggered out, quiet and lethal, their footsteps echoing through the silence.

Danny stayed rooted in the doorway, heart hammering. Christ. It's not just about boxing. It's never just about boxing. These men smell desperation and call it opportunity. He could still go in, confront Mickey, spit out everything. Instead, he watched.

Tyrell leaned over the ropes. "You think I can take him?"

"Maybe," Mickey said. "But fighting ain't about can. It's about should."

Tyrell's eyes narrowed. "You're dodging."

"And you're dodging the truth," Mickey fired back. "He wants to feed you to the machine. You're not ready yet."

Tyrell dropped to the floor, walked to the trash, and tossed Carmine's card in without hesitation. His voice was quieter now. "When I was nine… my mom's boyfriend used to lock me in the basement. Hours. Once left me two days with a flashlight and a box of crackers."

Mickey stayed silent, listening.

"By high school, I figured people either ignored you… or used you," Tyrell went on. "No one believed in you. Just survive." He looked Mickey straight in the eye. "So when Carmine talks about cameras and paydays, it don't sound like noise. It sounds like a way out."

Mickey shook his head, steady. "Kid, I've seen a hundred Carmine Russos. They don't see fighters. They see money. You fight now, it's for him—not you."

Tyrell's jaw flexed. "What if this is my moment?"

Mickey's voice softened. "You hit harder than I ever did. Learn faster. Feel the ring. But you gotta grow into it."

Danny's throat closed. He had waited years—his whole life—for Mickey to speak to him like that. To speak with care, with belief, with pride. But Mickey had saved those words for someone else's son. *Not me. Never me.*

"You always talk about me," Tyrell pressed. "How I gotta be ready. Take my time. But what about you? That last fight you had—the one everyone whispers about but you never talk about… How'd it feel?"

The gym went still. Mickey's face tightened. Finally, he whispered: "Like I was drowning."

Tyrell nodded. "You walked away in the dark, man. No lights, no goodbye. Not even for yourself."

"I didn't deserve a curtain call," Mickey muttered. "I had nothing left."

"Bullshit," Tyrell shot back. "You do now. You think this is just my moment? You're wrong. This fight, this run, this gym—it's your story too. You deserve better. Maybe you need to be ready to forgive yourself."

Mickey's eyes shone, glassy. His jaw worked. "When the hell did you get so damn smart?"

Tyrell smirked faintly. "I've got a good trainer. And you're walking into that ring with me."

He stepped forward and hugged Mickey. A real hug. Solid. Mickey froze, then wrapped his arms around him too.

Danny's stomach dropped. He couldn't watch another second.

He turned, slipped out the door. The bell jingled softly overhead, but neither Mickey nor Tyrell noticed.

On the street, Danny's pace quickened. Streetlights blurred through the wet in his eyes, but he didn't wipe them away. He just kept walking.

Danny remembered what it felt like to be hugged by his father. It had been a long time, but to Danny it felt almost like yesterday. All this time, he promised to keep the doors closed. *I will not be hurt the way Maria was. I'm different. Stronger. Safer.* Until he wasn't.

Seeing Mickey and Tyrell embrace brought back memories, a lot of good ones, during the happy times. Danny had tried to forge this version of Mickey from existence, to reduce him to nothing but mistakes and failures. But the truth was that this version scared him the most—the father who still had something to give. Because if Mickey could love someone else like that, then maybe he really had chosen not to love Danny.

And that was the deepest cut of all.

15

Flashbulbs and Shadows

The press room at the Boston Convention Center pulsed with anticipation. Rows of reporters leaned forward with recorders, cameras stacked three deep in the aisles. The Topline Promotions banner stretched across the stage, and under the hot lights, the fighters sat flanked by their handlers—Tyrell in a plain black hoodie, Seamus Doherty in a sharp gray suit with an Irish flag pin on the lapel, and between them, Carmine Russo glowing like a man who owned the room.

The PR rep, too young to hide the nerves in his voice, tapped the microphone.

"Ladies and gentlemen, thank you for being here today. On behalf of Topline Promotions, we're proud to announce the co-main event of the upcoming Boston Warzone card, four weeks from Saturday. An international clash between Seamus 'The Bear' Doherty and Tyrell Banks."

Flashes detonated like firecrackers. The sound of shutters was a steady storm.

Carmine leaned into the mic, grinning like the devil in a tuxedo. "Boston's about to find out the difference between loud and legendary. Seamus here is gonna turn this hype train into scrap metal."

Seamus sat forward, voice heavy with Dublin grit. "Tyrell's a good kid. Fast feet. Quick tongue. But that bell rings, and all I see is red. And when I see red, boys fall."

Reporters shouted over one another. One rose above the rest.

"Tyrell, you're young, barely out of the amateurs. Why take this fight now?"

Tyrell leaned into the mic, calm as stone. "Because I'm ready."

A ripple of reaction. Carmine chuckled into his mic. "Cute."

Another voice from the crowd: "Seamus, do you see him as a real threat?"

The Irishman smirked. "Threat? Nah. But every man bleeds if you hit him in the right spot. I'll find his spot."

The room broke into a low rumble. Cameras snapped.

Then came the question that sliced the air in two.

"Tyrell—will Mickey Brannigan be in your corner?"

Reporters leaned forward, hungry.

Tyrell didn't hesitate. "He's family. He'll be there."

Another blast of flashes, brighter than the last. A stir went through the crowd—Mickey Brannigan's name carried weight, even buried under decades of silence.

A veteran journalist raised his voice. "Mickey Brannigan—the same Brannigan who hasn't been seen on a major card since '9? The same Brannigan whose career ended on a loss?"

Murmurs rippled. Carmine smiled wider, scenting blood.

Tyrell didn't flinch. "Yeah. That Brannigan. And I'm proud of it."

"Some would say Mickey's past makes him a liability," another reporter pressed. "Why align yourself with a man who—"

Tyrell cut him off, voice sharp now. "Because he believes in me. That's more than any of you in this room ever did."

The words cracked across the microphones like a whip.

Carmine raised his eyebrows theatrically. "Careful, kid. Belief don't win fights. Power does."

Seamus leaned closer, eyes burning. "And power's what I've got. I plan on putting you down."

Tyrell's jaw set. He leaned into his own mic, voice steady and low. "Hope you bring your passport—'cause when I'm done, you're going home early."

The room exploded—shouts, laughter, the frantic storm of shutters. Carmine slapped the table, laughing like he'd just sold out the Garden himself.

"Now we got fireworks. Print that, boys. Write it big."

The PR rep, sweating now, rushed back to the podium. "The fight is official. Four weeks. TD Garden. Full card announcement coming soon. Thank you, everyone."

* * *

The press conference ended, but the tension didn't. Tyrell posed stiffly for photos, jaw tight, eyes forward. Seamus smiled for the cameras, Carmine's hand heavy on his shoulder.

When the cameras died down, Carmine leaned close to Tyrell, his voice a hiss. "You've got a mouth, kid. Let's see if you've got the chin to match it."

Tyrell didn't blink.

Outside, Boston's air cut sharp as knives. Tyrell stepped out of the convention center into the cold, exhaling steam. By the curb, Mickey stood waiting, hands shoved in his coat pockets.

"Well?" Mickey asked.

Tyrell let out a long breath. "It's on. Four weeks. You in?"

Mickey's grin broke through like an old scar reopened. "You couldn't keep me away if you tried."

* * *

Hours later, the conference replayed on local news stations. The broadcast flickered across Danny Brannigan's living room.

The screen showed Tyrell at the podium, calm, composed, Mickey's name spilling into the air like it still meant something. "He's family. He'll be there."

Danny sat on the couch, tie loosened, one hand pressed against his chin. The TV lit his face in bursts of camera flashes. His jaw stayed hard, but his eyes betrayed him—flickering with something between rage and longing.

On the screen, Carmine was laughing, Seamus was promising blood, and Mickey's name was back in circulation.

Upstairs, Caleb's lamp still glowed. The boy was under the covers, wide awake.

Danny stepped in, dropped a towel on the dresser, and sat on the edge of the bed. "You still awake?"

"Kind of," Caleb said.

Danny hesitated, staring at the floor.

"Was that really Grandpa on TV?" Caleb asked.

Danny's throat tightened. "Yeah. That was him."

Caleb pushed. "What was he like? When you were my age?"

Danny breathed deep, eyes fixed forward. "Larger than life. He had this energy—like he was always about to run through a wall. But he made you feel safe. Or at least like no one else could touch you."

"Then why don't you talk to him anymore?"

Danny's jaw clenched. "Because he left when I needed him. And by the time he tried to come back... I had already built a life around not needing him."

Caleb whispered. "But do you miss him?"

Danny paused a long time. "I don't know. Sometimes... maybe."

Caleb asked. "Do you think he misses you?"

Danny breathed again. Deeply. "yeah, I think he does."

Danny clicked the lamp off. The room fell into darkness, the muffled echo of the press conference still bleeding faintly from the television downstairs.

He sat alone at the kitchen table. His eyes kept drifting to the door.

When he was a boy, that door had been a source of dread. Every time it creaked open, he braced himself—what form of Mickey Brannigan was going to show up. The family man or the broken man?

And now, years later, the fear was different but it was still there. He didn't fear being hit or shouted down. Mickey never did those things to him. He feared something worse, that letting his father back in would open old wounds he'd spent a lifetime trying to stitch shut.

16

Junkyard Dogs

The junkyard looked like a graveyard for machines—rusted car frames jutting up like broken ribs, shards of windshield glass catching the last light of the afternoon like scattered diamonds.

Mickey and Tyrell were finishing the kind of training session nobody did anymore—flipping tires and throwing short, brutal body shots. Their breaths came in white clouds.

Mickey wiped sweat from his brow. He was breathing harder than he should have been. He tried to hide it, moving toward a metal barrel to steady himself, but a sharp pain caught him in the ribs. His face tightened.

Tyrell noticed.

"You good?"

"I'm fine," Mickey growled. "Hands up. We're not done."

But when they circled again and Tyrell snapped a quick jab, Mickey slipped too slow and stumbled. His knees buckled for a heartbeat.

"Dammit—hold up."

He leaned against a dented pickup, breath rattling in his chest.

Tyrell took a hesitant step closer.

"Take a second, Mick. It's fine."

"I said I'm fine."

But he grabbed his stomach in pain.

Tyrell saw it.

He hesitated—then said what he shouldn't have.

"The meds are supposed to help with that," he murmured.

Mickey froze.

A long, terrible silence spread between them.

"What did you say?" Mickey asked, his voice low and dangerous.

Tyrell's throat went dry. "I—wasn't snooping. I just… saw the bottle. In your room."

Mickey closed his eyes. There was a storm behind them.

"And you didn't think to mind your own damn business?"

"Mick—"

"You think I want the kid I'm training looking at me like I'm halfway in the ground?"

"That's not how I look at you."

Mickey finally turned. His breath came uneven. His voice was cracked porcelain.

"You weren't supposed to know," he said.

Tyrell swallowed. "Figured you'd tell me when you felt like it."

Mickey nodded once—barely.

When he spoke again, it was softer, but somehow more painful.

"A fighter only gets so many secrets he still owns."

Tyrell tried again. "Mick—"

"Don't say anything else, kid. Not now."

Mickey pushed himself upright and walked back toward the center of the yard, every step defiant against the pain.

"Come on," he barked. "Round's not over. If you're staying with me, you don't ease up. Ever."

Tyrell watched him—understanding more than he let on—then raised his hands.

"Then I won't," he said quietly.

They squared up again.

And the ground between them shifted—deeper, heavier, unspoken.

***

The nursing home was sometimes a surprising place of refuge.

Tyrell walked in holding a small paper bag. His eyes searched the room until they found her.

Grandma Evelyn sat hunched in an over-sized cardigan, watching a muted game show, her gaze drifting unfocused.

"Hey, Grandma," he said gently.

At first she didn't look up. Then her eyes lifted—cloudy, searching.

"Do I… know you?" she asked softly.

Tyrell forced a small smile.

"Yeah. It's me. Ty. I brought you something."

He set the bag on the table and pulled out the cornbread—wrapped carefully, like it might break.

"Figured you'd want some real food. Not the mush they serve here."

Evelyn sniffed the air and her face softened.

"Cornbread?"

"Your recipe," Tyrell said. "Best I could do."

She touched the container with trembling fingers—touching more memory than object.

"My Henry used to make that for me," she whispered.

Tyrell laughed sadly. "No, that was me. I used to make it after school. You always said I burned it."

Her brow furrowed. Searching inside her own mind.

Then she lifted her hand—slowly, uncertain—and touched his cheek.

Her fingers trembled.

And for a moment—just a moment—her eyes cleared.

"You're the boxer," she whispered.

Tyrell froze, breath catching.

"Yeah," he whispered. "Yeah, I'm the boxer."

"You always were," she said faintly. "Always fighting the world…"

The spark faded as quickly as it came. Her gaze drifted again.

"Cornbread smells burnt," she murmured.

Tyrell choked out a laugh, wiping his eye.

"Yeah. You always said that."

She settled back into her chair.

Tyrell pulled his shoulders in, trying to hold onto the gift she'd given him—that flicker of recognition he hadn't seen in months.

He stood, leaned down, and whispered,

"I'll come back tomorrow."

Evelyn smiled at him—not because she knew him, but because she felt safe.

"Thank you," she said.

Tyrell walked out blinking hard as the game-show buzzer sounded behind him.

* * *

The children's room was barely big enough for the two beds squeezed into it. Malik lay under the thin blankets, eyes half-closed, the way kids pretend to be asleep until the person they're waiting for finally shows.

Tyrell stood in the doorway, gym bag still on his shoulder, exhaustion weighing heavy on him—the kind that lived in bones, not muscles. But his expression softened when he saw his little brother curled up, trying to fight sleep.

"You still awake, lil man?" he whispered.

Malik nodded and slid over, making space. Tyrell sat on the edge of the bed, lowering himself slowly, careful not to shake the frame.

"You gonna win your first fight?" Malik asked, voice small, hopeful.

Tyrell smiled—not the cocky grin he threw around the neighborhood, but something gentler, honest.

"I'm gonna try my hardest," he said. "That's what I can promise."

Malik considered that, his brow creasing like he was weighing the answer.

"You scared?" he asked.

Tyrell exhaled. He could have lied. Maybe once he would have. Not tonight.

"Yeah," he said softly. "A little."

Tyrell shook his head and ruffled Malik's hair.

"It ain't the fight I'm scared of."

"Then what?" Malik whispered.

Tyrell looked at him—really looked—at the kid who saw him as something more than he ever saw in himself.

"Letting you down," Tyrell said.

Malik sat up a little, shaking his head so fast the blankets rustled.

"You never let me down," he said. "You're my hero, Ty."

The words hit him harder than any punch Mickey ever threw. Tyrell swallowed against the ache rising in his chest.

He pulled Malik into a light hug, careful not to crush him with strength or hope.

"Get some sleep," Tyrell murmured.

Malik nodded and snuggled deeper under the blankets, eyes following Tyrell as he stood to leave.

Tyrell reached for the light switch and flicked it off, plunging the room back into the soft, flickering glow of the nightlight.

Tyrell stepped into the hallway and gently closed the bedroom door behind him.

When he turned, he froze.

His mother stood at the far end of the hall—half-cast in darkness, one hand pressed over her mouth. She hadn't meant to overhear. But she had.

Her eyes glistened in the dim light, full of a thousand things she never had the time or the words to say.

She looked at him—really looked—at the son who had been forced to become a man far too early.

Tyrell held her gaze. He didn't speak. He didn't need to.

She turned away first, wiping her tears with the back of her hand as she slipped into her bedroom.

Tyrell watched her go, the weight settling deeper on his shoulders—a burden he carried, but also something like honor. Something like duty.

17

Help Me

Chopper sat hunched at his battered old desk, a chipped mug balanced in his hand.

A knock, low and uncertain, broke the silence.

"Door's open," Chopper muttered, without looking up.

The hinges creaked. Mickey stepped inside, his hoodie pulled low over his head. He looked older than the night before, pale and drawn, a sheen of sweat across his brow that had nothing to do with work. He eased the door closed and lowered himself into the chair across from Chopper with a wince, one hand pressed against his stomach. His breathing was shallow, like each inhale scraped against something sharp inside.

Chopper looked up, eyes narrowing. "You look worse than usual. That time of night again?"

Mickey exhaled through his nose, voice rough. "Couldn't sleep. Stomach's all twisted."

"You taking the meds?" Chopper asked.

"Some days," Mickey said with a shrug. "They just dull things. Doesn't stop what's coming."

Chopper leaned back, mug in hand, eyes steady. He'd seen too many fighters in this chair, all of them thinking they could out-stare death the same way they out-stared opponents. "It never does." He paused, let the weight settle. "But you're doing right by that kid."

Mickey shifted in his seat, restless. His fingers tapped against his thigh, nervous in a way his fists never had been. "I hope so. I made a lot of wrong turns. In the ring. Outside it. I don't wanna pass that down."

Chopper set his mug aside, leaning forward now, elbows on the desk. "Then don't."

Mickey looked up, almost startled.

"Teach him the best of you," Chopper said, his voice firm, almost gentle.

Mickey blinked, swallowing hard. The words hit somewhere deeper than he wanted to admit. His eyes burned but he forced the feeling down, tried to bury it under years of practiced toughness.

* * *

Danny didn't go straight home after school. He didn't even know where he was driving until the tires crunched across the gravel lot and the dark silhouette of St. Matthew's rose in his headlights. The church had been there since long before he was born, stone walls and a crooked steeple pressed against the night sky.

He killed the engine, sat for a long moment with his hands on the wheel, knuckles white, and finally stepped out.

The wooden doors creaked when he pulled them open. Inside, the sanctuary was dim, lit only by the faint glow of red votive candles flickering in the corner. The air smelled of old wood and wax. His footsteps echoed as he moved down the aisle and slipped into a pew halfway back.

He wasn't religious. Not in the slightest. But tonight, he needed somewhere to sit where silence didn't feel like defeat. Somewhere to ask questions he couldn't voice to his son, his colleagues, or even himself.

He clasped his hands together, not in prayer, just to keep them from trembling. The stained-glass windows loomed above, saints and angels bathed in moonlight. Their faces were calm, peaceful, certain. He envied them.

"Where were you?" he whispered, his voice swallowed by the cavernous dark. "Where were you when I needed you?"

Memories crowded in whether he wanted them or not. Sitting on the stoop as a boy, waiting for Mickey to come home. Maria's muffled crying behind a locked door. The phone that never rang the night Caleb was born. Maria's funeral, her picture framed in lilies, and Mickey nowhere in sight.

Danny felt abandoned. By his father. By God. By anyone who was supposed to care. He wanted to believe there was something more—someone listening. But belief felt like holding water in his hands: the tighter he gripped, the faster it slipped away.

Maria had been different. She was the faithful one, the one who believed every storm passed for a reason. She lit candles before dinner, whispered quiet prayers before bed. She told Danny once that faith was the only thing stronger than fear.

He wished he had that. He wished he could trust the silence the way she had.

Instead, he sat in the half-light, staring at the crucifix at the front of the church. The carved Christ hung there in eternal agony, arms stretched wide, head bowed.

"Mom believed in You," Danny murmured, his voice breaking. "Why can't I?"

The question drifted into the rafters and died. No voice answered. No warmth wrapped around him. Just the creak of the old building and the faint guttering of candles.

Danny pressed his hands to his face. For the first time in years, he wanted to believe. Not for himself, but for Caleb. For Maria. For the boy upstairs asking questions he didn't know how to answer.

He sat there a long while, alone in the dark, trying to bargain with a God he wasn't sure existed.

Finally, he stood, slid his hands into his pockets, and walked back down the aisle. The door groaned shut behind him, leaving the church to its shadows and silence.

Out in the night air, he whispered one last thing, so quiet even he wasn't sure if he'd said it out loud.

"Help me."

***

The church was still heavy on him when he left—the smell of candles, the weight of silence, the kind of quiet that followed you even into the street. Danny drove without thinking, ending up in Arlington.

He pushed open the door to a corner bar. The place was half-empty, just a couple of guys hunched over the Celtics game on TV and a jukebox humming low. Danny slid onto a stool and nodded to the bartender.

"Whiskey," he said. His voice came out rough, like gravel in his throat.

The glass hit the counter with a soft clink. Amber liquid sloshed, catching the dim light. Danny wrapped his hand around it and just stared.

It would be easy. Too easy. One drink to take the edge off. One drink to forget the tightness in his chest every time he thought of Mickey. He thought about his father in dingy bars, hunched over glasses just like this one, chasing silence at the bottom.

Danny's reflection wavered in the drink. Same jawline. Same tired eyes. For a moment, it felt like he was looking at Mickey instead of himself.

"Christ," he muttered under his breath.

His hand tightened, then loosened. He pushed the glass back across the counter. "Not tonight," he said.

The bartender gave a shrug, sliding the glass away. Danny stood, the stool scraping across the floor. He shoved his hands into his jacket pockets and walked out into the cold night air, lungs filling like he'd just escaped something bigger than the bar itself.

For a moment, he let himself believe he'd chosen the one thing his father never could—walking away.

***

Lexington, Massachusetts. Calm and quiet. Trees swayed outside Jackie's colonial home, their shadows stretching across the lawn. Inside, a fire crackled low in the brick hearth.

Danny sat on the edge of an armchair, hands clasped tight, jaw working like he was chewing on something heavier than words. Across from him, Jackie curled into the couch, legs folded underneath her, mug of tea in hand.

"You wanna tell me why you've looked like someone stole your soul since you walked in?" she asked softly.

Danny exhaled. "I saw him."

She didn't need to ask who.

"At the gym. Just watched him walking out after training that kid. He looked… older. Smaller than I remember."

"He is," Jackie said, her voice quiet. "Older. Sicker."

Danny's eyes flicked up, sharp. "How long have you known?"

Her gaze sank into her tea. "Few weeks. He showed up here, told me six months. Maybe less. Pancreatic cancer."

"Yeah," Danny answered, his voice flat. "I saw him a few months ago."

"He's trying, Danny. In his own Mickey-Brannigan-stubborn kind of way."

Danny gave a short, bitter laugh. "Trying doesn't erase twenty years of bullshit."

Her eyes softened. "He is dying, Danny."

Danny stared at the floor, jaw tightening. "He may be dying. But to me he died a long time ago."

"You think I don't know that?" Jackie said, her voice rising just a touch. "He punishes himself every day—and not in some noble, poetic way. Just… quietly."

Danny's eyes flickered, then dropped again. He was listening, even if he didn't want to admit it.

"Danny," she pressed gently. "He lost parts of himself—the good parts—when life hit too hard."

He rubbed his jaw, eyes distant. "You think I'm cold?"

"I think you're afraid," Jackie said. "And I don't blame you. But Caleb's going to ask questions one day. And what are you going to say? That you had a chance to speak with your father before he died and you walked away?" She leaned forward, her gaze steady. "You don't have to forgive him. You don't even have to like him. But don't let your silence write the ending."

Danny clenched his jaw until it ached. "What if I don't have anything left to say?"

"Then just listen," Jackie said softly. "Because he has plenty. And it might be the only time you ever hear him say it."

She reached across the space and placed a hand on his arm, squeezing gently.

"He might not be a good father, Danny," she added. "But he's trying to die as one."

Danny's eyes began to sting, moisture gathering at the edges, but he refused to let the tears fall. Jackie didn't push him further. She rose quietly, touched his shoulder as she passed, and slipped out the door.

The house was silent again except for the faint crackle of the fire. Danny leaned forward and picked up his phone. For a long moment, he just stared at the screen.

He hesitated. Locked the phone. Set it down.

He wasn't ready. But maybe… soon.

18

The Empty Ring

Tyrell opened the front door to find Mickey standing there.

"Hey," Tyrell said, relief flickering across his face. "Thanks for coming."

Mickey stepped inside without ceremony, the faint smell of cold air trailing him. "You said come over. Thought maybe you were having second thoughts."

Tyrell grinned, though there was a nervous twitch to it. "Can I ask you something? And you gotta tell me the truth."

"Yeah, what's up?"

Tyrell hesitated, then exhaled. "Did you ever… I dunno… panic? Like right before a fight?"

Mickey chuckled, low and dry. "You mean like wanting to fake an injury and run out the back door?"

Tyrell laughed, embarrassed. "Yeah."

"Only once," Mickey said. His voice softened. "My first title shot. I was young, hadn't lost in five years. I was scared that night."

Tyrell's eyebrows shot up. "Come on. You?"

"Me," Mickey said firmly. "I kept thinking, what if this is all I am? What if I lose, and they forget my name by Sunday?"

Tyrell leaned forward, his voice barely above a whisper. "What happened?"

Mickey leaned back into the couch, eyes narrowing at the memory. "I got dropped in the third. Hard body shot—felt like my lungs were gonna pop. I got up at eight. Heard Chopper screaming from the corner, 'You came this far just to fold?' Something flipped in me right then."

Tyrell nodded slowly, absorbing every word. "So fear doesn't mean you're weak?"

"No," Mickey said. "Fear's a map. Points you toward what matters."

Tyrell's voice cracked a little. "What if I lose?"

"Then you lose," Mickey said gently. "And you get back up. Most men don't ever even get the chance."

The silence that followed was heavy, not awkward but sacred. Tyrell's eyes shone with emotion. "I don't know if I'm ready."

Mickey leaned forward, his tone firm, unshakable. "You're ready."

"How do you know?"

"Because you called me tonight," Mickey said. "You didn't want answers—you wanted the truth."

Tyrell swallowed, his throat tight. "Thanks for not dying before this."

Mickey smiled through the pain, the kind that lived in his bones now. "I told you. One more round."

They locked eyes, neither blinking, until Mickey stood. He reached out and set a heavy hand on Tyrell's shoulder—solid, grounding, almost fatherly.

For Tyrell, it was enough.

* * *

Later that night, Mickey found himself in Boston, his old sedan parked a block away from TD Garden. The city was alive around him—traffic lights flashing red and green across wet pavement, the low rumble of the T under his feet, the distant chatter of bar crowds pouring into the street. It was all noise, all motion, but Mickey felt apart from it. Like the world had already moved on without him, and he was just drifting through its edges.

The night wind cut sharp off the Charles, whipping his hoodie tight around his face as he stood before the arena's glass facade. Above him, a massive banner snapped and flapped in the gusts:

BANKS VS. DOHERTY—THIS SATURDAY

Tyrell's face was plastered on one side, young and hungry, fists raised, eyes lit with fire. On the other, Seamus Doherty, tough and brutal, the challenger from across the sea. Between them, bold block letters promised violence, spectacle, a war Boston hadn't seen in years

Mickey's chest rose and fell, slow. He wasn't on the banner, not even in the fine print at the bottom. But part of him didn't need to be.

He tugged his jacket closer and stepped toward the doors. The lone security guard at the entrance looked him over, recognized the face—older now, grayer, but still unmistakable—and wordlessly waved him through.

Empty seats stretched endlessly in the shadows, tier after tier climbing toward the rafters. And at the center of it all, lit by a single overhead spotlight like a holy altar, was the ring. Four ropes. Neutral corners. The square that had given him everything and taken more.

Mickey walked down the aisle slowly, every footstep echoing. When he reached the apron, he paused. For a moment, he just looked at it—this simple square of canvas that had once been the whole world. Then, with deliberate care, he climbed between the ropes.

Inside, it was different. It always was. The outside world fell away. The ring was its own country, and for a long time, Mickey had been its citizen, its champion, its sacrifice.

He brushed his hand across the top rope, rough tape against his skin, and closed his eyes. The ghosts came fast. Cheers and boos, blood and sweat. Choppers voice barking from the corner. Maria's face, glowing in the crowd, smiling as though she believed in him more than he ever believed in himself. Danny's silence, heavier than any punch he ever took.

"I left too much of myself in here," he whispered. His voice cracked in the hollow arena.

He dropped to one knee, his body slow, stiff. The canvas creaked beneath him like it remembered the weight. Memories rushed in—his father's funeral, Chopper's tough love, Maria's hands patching cuts he couldn't hide.

He bowed his head. Not in prayer—he hadn't prayed in years. But in surrender.

Tomorrow wasn't about belts or money, not about rankings or headlines. It was about redemption. Not the kind the crowd handed out with applause, but the kind you left behind like a footprint in the dirt. For Danny, who still carried wounds with his name on them. For Tyrell, who deserved a better future than Mickey ever had. For Maria, whose faith had carried them both further than he realized.

He stood, slower now, joints aching, chest tight, and looked around at the vast emptiness of the seats. In his mind they were full the roar of Boston rising, a sound that had once belonged to him.

"Tomorrow," he whispered, voice trembling but steady, "we finish it right."

He lingered one last moment, drinking it in, before slipping through the ropes. His feet hit the floor hard. The sound echoed.

Mickey walked back up the aisle, the spotlight shrinking behind him until the ring was swallowed by darkness. He didn't look back.

Because the next time he crossed those ropes, it would be for the last time.

* * *

Tyrell sat on the edge of his bed, hands clasped so tight his knuckles whitened. The house was quiet except for the faint hum of the street outside. His gear bag sat in the corner, gloves folded neatly on top. He should've been sleeping, but instead he found himself staring at the ceiling, a weight in his chest he couldn't shake.

He hadn't prayed in years. Not since he was six, kneeling by the side of his bed while his mom whispered words over him. Back then, his prayer had been simple: Please let this man who moved in be the father I need. Please let him stay, please don't let him leave, please don't let him hurt her. That prayer had gone unanswered, and Tyrell had carried the silence like a scar ever since.

But tonight, something pulled him back to it. Maybe it was the way Mickey's hands shook when he thought nobody noticed, or the cough he tried to cover with a laugh, or just the raw truth hanging over them both: Mickey didn't have much time.

Tyrell bowed his head. His voice cracked as he whispered, "God… I don't even know if you hear me anymore. I don't even know if I'm supposed to talk to you like this. But if you do… don't let him go yet. Don't let Mickey leave before he sees me win."

He swallowed hard, eyes burning. "I don't care about me. I don't care about the fight. I just… I need him to see it. I need him to know that everything he gave me wasn't wasted."

Silence answered. But for the first time since he was a boy, Tyrell felt something shift inside him—not peace, not certainty, but the strange comfort of having said it out loud, to someone, anyone.

He lay back slowly, hands still folded on his chest, and closed his eyes.

* * *

Mickey left the arena and found himself walking through the city like he had a hundred times before. Boston's air was damp, carrying the smell of the harbor and the faint tang of beer from bars spilling their last patrons onto the sidewalks.

His boots carried him toward Chopper's Gym, almost on instinct. It was a walk he knew by heart, one that had carried him from boyhood sparring sessions to title fights, from nights of triumph to nights of regret.

The streets hadn't changed. The cracked sidewalks, the flicker of the streetlamps, the way the wind funneled down the alleys—they were the same as they had been when he was young, hungry, fists wrapped tight and heart beating like a drum. What had changed were the people. The dockworkers with rolled-up sleeves had been replaced by kids in hoodies and earbuds. The old corner diners were now late-night pizza joints. But the streets themselves—they kept their secrets. They remembered.

Mickey slowed in front of a boarded-up storefront where he once celebrated a win, drunk on youth and promise. He could still see the ghost of his reflection in the glass, the young man he used to be, swaggering and unbreakable. Now, in the same pane, he saw the slope of his shoulders, the gray at his temples, the lines etched deep around his mouth.

And yet, the walk comforted him. It reminded him he still belonged here, that the city knew him, even if most of its people had forgotten. Boston had watched him rise, and it would watch him fall. The streets didn't care who you were, but they never lied.

As he neared the sign of Chopper's Gym, Mickey exhaled. He was home— not in a house, not in a bed, but in the rhythm of these streets, the only place that had never turned its back on him.

19

Fight Night

The bass-thump of the crowd above felt like distant thunder. TD Garden vibrated—sold out, standing room only. A sea of anticipation waited on the other side of the tunnel, the kind of anticipation that felt alive, breathing, hungry.

Mickey Brannigan walked in first, Chopper beside him, their shoes clicking against the concrete floor. They had made this walk more times than either could count—Madison Square Garden, Caesars Palace, the old Boston Garden. Nights of glory. Nights of heartbreak. Nights where the air smelled of blood and roses, where the lights burned so bright you couldn't see the future.

Once, they had been the men the world came to see. Now, they moved slower, older, shadows of the men they had been. But ritual was ritual, and this walk still belonged to them. Every step felt like it carried a thousand echoes. Every step reminded Mickey he was still here, still part of something that had defined his entire life.

When they reached the locker room, the noise died away. The world outside was chaos; inside, it was silence.

* * *

Danny hadn't planned on coming.

He told himself all day he wouldn't. That he had papers to grade, Caleb's hockey practice to worry about, anything else but this. But when the sun went down, his car seemed to find its own way onto I-93, the lights of Boston pulling him in like a tide.

By the time he reached Causeway Street, the sidewalks were packed—fans spilling out of bars, lines curling around the arena, the buzz of fight night electrifying the air. Danny felt it in his bones—the same current he had felt as a boy, holding Maria's hand in old arenas.

He kept his head down, ticket clenched in his hand. He felt like an intruder, as if every face in the crowd somehow knew who he was—the son of Mickey Brannigan, the ghost whose name still echoed in this city. What if someone recognized him? Would they see a fan, or just the proof of Mickey's failures made flesh?

When he reached his row, Jackie was already there. She rose and hugged him without a word, her eyes searching his face, as if to make sure he was really here. Danny just nodded and sat down, his chest tight.

And then the lights dropped. The arena inhaled as one.

Danny looked up, heart pounding, just as the tunnel across the floor burst with red and white strobes. Tyrell bounced into view, fists raised, Mickey a step behind him. The crowd detonated.

For Danny, the years fell away. The sound, the lights, the sight of his father stepping toward the ring—older now, slower, but still carrying that impossible weight—slammed into him like a punch to the ribs.

He had sworn he'd never come back here. Never let this world touch him again.

And yet, here he was.

Watching.

* * *

Tyrell sat on the bench, fists wrapped tight, chin low, locked into stillness. Black trunks with deep red trim hugged his frame—a quiet homage to

109

Mickey's championship colors in '86. His breathing was steady, but his eyes flicked to Mickey every few seconds, like a soldier waiting for orders before battle.

Mickey stood over him, tightening the gloves with practiced precision. His hands trembled slightly, but his face was steel.

"You ready?" Mickey asked, voice low.

Tyrell nodded.

"Not fight ready," Mickey said. "I mean ready. For everything. The lights. The noise. The pain."

Tyrell looked up, jaw set. "I ain't scared."

Mickey's mouth bent into a faint grin. "That ain't what I asked."

For a moment Tyrell faltered, then lifted his chin higher. "I'm ready."

Mickey cupped the back of his neck, firm like a father. Their eyes locked. Two men from different worlds, different eras, bound by something deeper than boxing.

From the doorway, Chopper leaned against the frame, arms crossed, towel slung over his shoulder. His eyes were misty but proud. He gave Mickey a small nod.

"It's time."

***

The arena went dark.

A low hum rolled through the crowd, swelling into a roar. Lights exploded over the ring, turning the canvas into a glowing altar.

"And now," the announcer's voice boomed, "entering the arena… accompanied by former World Champion Mickey Brannigan… Tyrell Banks!"

The tunnel lit with red and white strobes. Tyrell bounced gently, eyes forward. But it was Mickey who drew the first eruption. As he stepped into view, the ovation cracked like thunder—not nostalgia, but reverence.

He wore a dark coat, collar high, hat low. A gladiator out of time. His gait was slower now, deliberate, each step echoing every fight, every loss, every regret. This walk—his last walk—belonged to him.

He didn't wave. He didn't smile. He absorbed it. Soaking it all in. This was his curtain call, whether the world knew it or not.

At ringside, Mickey stopped, staring at the canvas. This ring had made him, broken him, defined him. And maybe now, it would complete him. For a heartbeat he hesitated. Then, with a sharp breath, he climbed between the ropes.

Tyrell stood in his corner, bouncing lightly, shaking out his arms. Across from him, Seamus Doherty—lean, brutal, unbeaten—rolled his neck, eyes cold. Between flashes of the stare-down, he smirked and wiped his nose with a gloved thumb, like a man savoring a meal he hadn't yet eaten.

Mickey gripped Tyrell's shoulders. "This is your night and it's your time."

Tyrell swallowed hard. "Let's do this, Mick."

The lights dimmed further. The crowd inhaled as one.

The bell clanged.

Round One.

Tyrell stormed forward, nerves burning, adrenaline spitting fire through his veins. Seamus met him instantly. A jab cracked his chin. Another jab. Then a savage hook—Tyrell hit the ropes hard.

"Circle! Legs!" Mickey barked.

But the moment swallowed him whole. Seamus swarmed—lefts, rights, an uppercut. One slipped through. Tyrell staggered. Then—boom—down.

Danny lurched halfway out of his seat in Section 112. Jackie grabbed his arm. The roar shook the rafters.

"One… two… three…" the ref counted.

Mickey's voice cut like a knife. "Get up, Ty! This ain't your ending!"

Seven. Tyrell rose, legs shaky but spirit burning.

The fight resumed. Seamus grinned, sensing weakness. Tyrell moved more carefully, blocking, jabbing, clinging to Mickey's voice. The bell saved him.

Back in the corner, Mickey wiped sweat from his neck. "You hear me? You don't win it all at once. Chip away. One second at a time. Trust your legs. Trust your chin. But most of all, trust your heart."

Tyrell nodded, blood at the corner of his mouth. "I got him. He's a tank, but I'm smarter."

Round two.

Tyrell breathed steadier now. He jabbed, circled. Seamus clipped him with a right hand, but he stayed upright. Survived.

By round three, he caught Seamus with a snapping uppercut. The crowd roared.

Danny leaned forward, jaw tight. Jackie whispered, "He's figuring him out."

Rounds blurred. In the fifth, Tyrell ducked under an uppercut, countered to the ribs. The tide shifted. In the sixth, Seamus staggered him again, proving the danger was real. The seventh was war, sweat and blood flying, neither man giving an inch.

By round eight, Tyrell moved looser, dancing smart, snapping the jab, fighting like the ring belonged to him.

Then came round nine. Seamus hammered him with a right hand that would've finished most men. Tyrell's head snapped back, his knees wobbled— but he smiled through the blood.

The crowd exploded. Mickey slammed his fists against the ropes. "Stay the course!" The bell clanged. Both men staggered to their corners, wrecked but unbroken.

Danny leaned forward, elbows on his knees, chest tight. He had been here before. Not in this exact seat, not in this exact fight—but as a boy, clinging to Maria's hand, wide-eyed as Mickey Brannigan stepped into the ring. He remembered the smells, the sounds, the way the bell was both a promise and a threat.

And as he watched Tyrell now—long arms pumping, stubborn chin refusing to quit, fighting not with polish but with fire—it was like watching his father all over again.

Tyrell was raw, imperfect. But there was something in the way he refused to back down, something reckless but beautiful, that carried Mickey's shadow.

For the first time, Danny didn't just see Mickey as the broken man who had left. He saw the ghost of the fighter Mickey used to be—alive again through Tyrell.

His throat tightened. Jackie glanced at him, but he didn't speak. His eyes stayed locked on the corner.

Mickey stood there, jaw locked, hands gripping the ropes, whispering with all he had left. His voice shook with pride, with fear, and with something Danny had convinced himself Mickey never had—love.

And in that moment, Danny realized: this wasn't just Tyrell's fight. It was Mickey's. It always had been.

Danny had spent years convincing himself Mickey never loved anyone but himself. But what he saw in the corner now—an old fighter, jaw clenched, whispering like a man desperate to give this kid the ending he never had—broke something in him.

For the first time in years, Danny wondered if Mickey had always been more than the man who walked away.

20

The Walk Back

Danny Brannigan sat in his seat at TD Garden, the crowd's rumble pounding in his chest like a second heartbeat. The sound wasn't just noise—it was alive, a pulse that carried him backward through time. For a fleeting moment, he wasn't a man in his late thirties—he was just a young kid again, legs dangling off the couch in his Boxford home. Bowls of popcorn in their laps. His mother sitting cross-legged on the rug, eyes locked on the screen.

Maria had loved the greats—Hagler, Leonard, Hearns—but she believed in Mickey most. Danny remembered the way she leaned forward every time Mickey got clipped, muttering prayers under her breath like she could will him back up with sheer force of love. He remembered the smell of her hair when she hugged him after a win, the warmth of her arms that felt like armor against the world.

Those nights had felt sacred. Not just boxing. Family. The only time it had ever felt whole. The only time Mickey belonged to them both.

Now, looking down at the ring, Danny felt that ache stir again. Tyrell paced in his corner, bouncing lightly, and Danny saw Mickey in every move. The way he set his feet. The way his chin tucked tight behind his shoulder. A ghost flickering back to life.

Across the canvas, Mickey leaned close to Tyrell, adjusting his mouth guard with trembling hands. His fingers shook, but his voice was steady, as if he had found strength in the boy where his own body had failed him.

114

"Listen to me," Mickey rasped. "Keep that left hand high—he's leaning heavy on the counter. Don't go headhunting. Work the body first. Make him drop his hands, then you go upstairs. Don't chase it. Let it come to you."

Tyrell nodded, chest heaving, eyes locked on Mickey like every word was oxygen.

DING!

Round ten. The last round.

Tyrell rose from his stool, lungs burning, gloves heavy as anchors. His legs felt like bricks, but his eyes—his eyes were sharp. Across the ring, Seamus Doherty cracked his neck and stormed forward. He was battered, his right eye swollen shut, mouth bloodied, but still dangerous.

The bell rang for the tenth and final round. The TD Garden rattled with noise, a storm contained in four walls. For the first thirty seconds, Tyrell kept his distance, working behind the jab, circling, measuring. Seamus pressed forward, cutting off the ring with heavy steps, looking for a kill shot.

The crowd swelled with every exchange. Every gasp and roar fed oxygen into his lungs.

At the one-minute mark, Tyrell saw his opening. Seamus lunged with a looping hook, and Tyrell slipped it, countering with a short left to the body. The shot landed deep, and Seamus grunted, backing up.

"That's it!" Mickey's voice cut through the din, rough but commanding from the corner. "That's the spot! Go back to the ribs!"

Tyrell pressed. Doubled the jab. Feinted low, then ripped a right cross upstairs that smacked flush against Seamus's jaw. The Garden erupted.

Seamus staggered. Tyrell smelled blood. His chest heaved like a furnace, but his mind narrowed to a pinpoint.

Midway through the round, Tyrell uncorked a flurry—jab, cross, hook, hook, uppercut, straight right. Seamus's guard split, his back hitting the ropes. Tyrell didn't rush. He reset, breathing hard, eyes cold. Control the fire. Don't let it burn you first.

Mickey's voice again, calm now, steady as stone. "Finish it like a technician."

Tyrell jabbed low, dragging Seamus's gloves down. Then he whipped a right hook upstairs, snapping Seamus's head to the side. And then—like lightning—he pivoted and delivered a left hook to the temple.

CRACK.

Seamus crumpled to the canvas, flat on his back, eyes glazed.

The Garden shook with the roar.

The referee dropped to his knees. "ONE! TWO!"

From ringside, Carmine Russo's voice cut through, frantic. "No… no, no, no, no…"

"THREE! FOUR! FIVE!"

Seamus rolled to his side, pawing for the ropes, too hurt, too slow.

"SIX! SEVEN! EIGHT! NINE! TEN!" The referee waved it off, gesturing with both arms. "That's it! It's over!"

The bell clanged over the din.

"Ladies and gentlemen," the announcer's voice thundered through the arena, "the winner by knockout—in the tenth round—TYRELL BANKS!"

The crowd exploded. Tyrell's knees nearly buckled with joy. He lifted his arms, screaming at the rafters. Mickey was already rushing into the ring, his old towel still around his neck, eyes wet. Tyrell grabbed him, shouting, "We did it! We really did it!"

Mickey pulled his forehead against Tyrell's, gripping the back of his head like a father. His voice broke. "You did more than that. You became."

They embraced, and for Mickey, the win wasn't about titles, money, or headlines. It was release. It was closure. It was finally giving what he couldn't give Danny—belief without conditions.

From the stands, Danny stood. Not cheering, not shouting—just clapping slowly, eyes locked on the man in the ring. His chest ached with something he didn't know how to name.

Reporters swarmed, microphones in faces, flashes blinding.

"Tyrell," one shouted, "first pro win, by knockout. How does it feel?"

Tyrell, still panting, sweat dripping down his face, grinned wide. "That win's not just mine. It's for every kid who ever felt alone… and for the man who saw something in me before I saw it in myself."

He turned, grabbed Mickey's wrist, and hoisted it high. "This one's for Mickey Brannigan!"

The Garden roared again, louder than ever.

* * *

Later, in the hallway beneath the arena, Tyrell walked beside Mickey. His hands were still wrapped, Mickey's old towel draped around his neck like a medal. They moved slow, through the crush of handshakes and cheers, into the dimmer quiet.

Mickey stopped suddenly. Tyrell glanced over. "You good?"

"Yeah," Mickey said, catching his breath. "Just… give me a second."

He turned toward the stands. Across the distance, he locked eyes with Danny. The crowd noise dulled, fading to nothing. For the first time in years, father and son didn't look away.

Danny shifted forward slightly, unbuttoned his coat, his hands falling loose at his sides.

Mickey straightened, shoulders pulling back, fatigue dropping away just for a moment. A long beat hung between them. Then Mickey gave a single nod—the kind of nod a father gives when words would only ruin it.

Tyrell followed Mickey's gaze, frowning in curiosity. "Who was that?"

Mickey smiled faintly, eyes still on Danny. "That's the last fight I gotta win."

Then he turned, and together, he and Tyrell disappeared down the tunnel.

Mickey felt the Garden's roar still humming through the floor, but it wasn't for him anymore. It belonged to Tyrell. And that was right. That was good.

He pulled the towel around his neck and walked slowly down the tunnel, each step echoing against the concrete. For years, the spotlight had been his. Tonight, he was just a shadow trailing behind a rising star.

Yet there was no bitterness. Only a heavy mix of pride and loss. Pride, because Tyrell had done what he always believed he could. Loss, because every fighter eventually makes their last walk.

The torch was passed.

21

One Final Fight

The diner sat half-empty. A plate of fries had been pushed to the side; two coffee cups sat cooling between them.

Tyrell leaned back in his seat, bruised and glowing with the high that came after a win—not just adrenaline, but something deeper, something earned. Sweat still clung faintly to him.

Across from him, Mickey looked pale. His breath was steady, but his shoulders slumped with an exhaustion he never admitted. Still, his eyes were alive. Quiet pride flickered there.

The check slid onto the table.

Tyrell grabbed it before Mickey could reach.

"Nah," he said, grinning. "This one's mine. Told you I'd cover the next meal."

He pulled out a small wad of bills—his fight money, crumpled from being shoved into his jeans pocket. He flattened the bills with his thumb and dropped them on the table.

Mickey shook his head, half amused, half warning.

"Careful," he muttered. "Money disappears faster than your hands do."

"I earned it," Tyrell shrugged. "Might as well feed the old man who got me here."

The joke softened something between them. Mickey smirked. Let it go.

Silence settled in—not awkward, not heavy. Something being exchanged without language. A kind of passing of fire.

Tyrell broke it softly.

"You were right," he said. "It ain't about speed. It's about rhythm."

Mickey met his eyes. For a moment he looked like he might say something more—something real—but instead he lifted his coffee and took a slow sip, his breath warming the rising steam.

Tyrell leaned forward, elbows on the table.

"So what's next?"

Mickey didn't answer immediately. His gaze drifted toward the window, to the empty street outside where a neon sign flickered with stubborn life. Rain tapped faintly against the glass.

When he finally spoke, his voice was low.

"Next round's yours."

Tyrell absorbed the weight of that—the acknowledgment, the promise, the burden. No jokes, no grin, no swagger. Just understanding.

* * *

Mickey Brannigan's battered sedan coughed into silence outside the gym. He stepped out, moving slower than he wanted to admit. Not just from age. From everything. From the fight. From the sickness. From years that never gave back what they took. His breath fogged in the cold morning air, shallow and uneven.

The gym door waited ahead, dark and quiet under the streetlight. But Mickey stopped short. Danny was standing there. His son. The sight froze him. Mickey's breath caught in his chest. He tried to play it off with a weak smile.

"You waiting for the sunrise," he asked softly, "or just trying to block the old man from getting in?"

"Neither," Danny said quietly.

Mickey looked down, the joke dying in his throat. This wasn't one of those mornings. His heart hammered against his ribs like he was walking into a title fight.

"I watched you last night," Danny continued. His voice carried the weight of someone who'd been turning words over for years, waiting for the right time. "And I realized something. You were never perfect. You were never even consistent. But when you believed in someone… you really believed in them. And I think maybe that scared the hell out of you."

Mickey's chest tightened. He lowered his head, his voice rough. "I don't got much time left, Danny."

"I know," Danny said.

"I'm sorry."

"I know," Danny whispered back. He hesitated, then added, "But I also know what she said. On the last day."

Mickey's shoulders tensed. He couldn't ask. He couldn't bear to.

"She said she loved you," Danny continued, his voice steadier now. "Even then. Even after everything."

Mickey broke. His face cracked, tears pushing hot into his eyes. "She shouldn't have. I didn't deserve it."

"Probably not," Danny said with a faint, sad shrug. "But I think you loved us the only way you knew how—by running toward something you thought would save you and running from the thing that actually could have."

Mickey's voice dropped to a ragged whisper. "What if I don't know how to stop?"

"Then you learn," Danny said firmly. He paused, searching his father's face. "I used to watch that clip, you know. The one from 1986. Right after the fight, when you ran into the crowd and picked me up. I was just a kid… but I remember thinking my dad was a goddamn superhero."

Mickey shook his head, his voice breaking. "I wish I could get those years back, kid."

Danny took a breath. "Come home. Meet your grandson."

Mickey wiped at his eyes, trembling now, silent. "You sure?"

"No," Danny said honestly. "But I know Mom would want us to try."

Mickey leaned back against the gym wall. His eyes shut tight, tears streaming freely now—not the shameful kind, but the kind that sounded like relief. Years of guilt pouring out, draining from him like poison.

Danny stepped closer. They didn't hug. They didn't need to. They just stood side by side, shoulder to shoulder, the space between them finally gone.

"You know," Mickey said through his tears, "she used to hum to me when I was cutting weight. Your mom. Didn't matter how weak I felt—I'd hear her from the hallway. Like she was saying, You're not done yet."

Danny's voice softened. "Maybe she still is."

For a long moment they stood there, father and son. Then, slowly, they began to walk. Not fast. Not apart. But together. Toward healing. Toward home.

* * *

Later that afternoon, Chopper sat hunched behind his battered desk, sorting through old papers with his reading glasses perched halfway down his nose. The ticking of the wall clock filled the silence like a metronome.

A soft knock came at the door. He looked up.

"Yeah?"

The door opened. Mickey stepped in, hesitating in the doorway like he wasn't sure he belonged.

"I'm heading out," Mickey said quietly.

Chopper nodded. They shared a long look—years of history packed into a single beat.

"Just..." Mickey cleared his throat. "Keep an eye on the kid, will ya?"

Chopper let out a rough chuckle.

"I'm an old man, Mick. Don't know how many eyes I got left."

Mickey almost smiled.

"But after everything you taught him..." Chopper continued, voice softening. "I don't think he needs much. He's gonna be fine. Gonna be a world champion someday—because of you."

Mickey looked down, his throat tightening, moved but trying not to show it. He turned to go.

"Hey," Chopper said softly. Mickey stopped in the doorway. "You did good, Mick."

Mickey held his breath. Then he nodded once, a simple, quiet acknowledgment. "Thank you, Chop."

22

Last Round

Mickey Brannigan drove slow through the crooked Boston streets, hands loose on the wheel, eyes flicking from the road to the rearview mirror. The reflection staring back at him wasn't a fighter anymore. His face had thinned, hollow at the cheeks, skin stretched over bone. His eyes still carried a glint, but it flickered now, faint, like a bulb about to burn out.

Every turn of the wheel felt like a choice. He had walked into world title fights with less nerves than this drive. It wasn't punches he feared. Or pain. Not even death. It was Danny—seeing his son face-to-face, no crowd to drown the silence, no bell to save him from what came next.

The world really was a crazy place. For years he had told himself his time with Danny had passed—that whatever bridge once stood between them had long been burned to ash. But now here he was, steering straight toward him, heart rattling like loose change in a pocket.

And in some quiet place in his chest, another thought lingered: *Maybe I was saving the best for last.*

His car coughed and shuddered to a stop in front of a two-story with white siding and blue shutters. A neat yard. A porch swing. A life.

Mickey shut off the engine, gripping the wheel one last time like it was the final set of ropes he'd ever hold. Then he let go.

* * *

The walkway stretched out in front of him, longer than any ring walk he'd ever made. His legs felt heavy, each step echoing like another round survived. At the door, he hesitated, knuckles hovering just short of wood. His chest burned.

Before he could knock, the door swung open.

Danny stood there in a T-shirt and jeans, his face older but not hard, his eyes carrying that guarded warmth—the look of a man who had decided to try.

"Hey," Danny said, almost awkward.

"Hey, Danny" Mickey replied, his voice low, husky.

"Come on in," Danny said, stepping aside.

But before Mickey could move, a smaller voice piped up from inside.

"Dad! Who's here?"

Footsteps pattered, and a boy appeared—a tall eleven-year-old with sandy hair and curious eyes that struck Mickey like a clean jab. For a second, his breath caught. It was Danny again, all those years ago—the same jaw, the same stubborn curiosity.

Caleb.

The boy slowed, staring at the stranger in the cap. "Who's that?"

Danny smiled faintly, resting a hand on his son's shoulder. "Caleb, this is your grandfather. Mickey Brannigan."

Caleb's eyes widened. "The fighter?"

Mickey chuckled softly, the sound cracked but genuine. "That's me, kiddo. Well… I used to be."

Danny added, "Not just any fighter. Your grandfather was the champion of the world."

"Champion of the world," Caleb whispered, almost in awe.

And just like that, Mickey was pulled backward—Danny no older than Caleb chasing toy cars across the carpet, pausing only when the TV replayed one of Mickey's knockouts. Maria in the kitchen stirring spaghetti, humming under her breath. Danny touching the belt like it was gold.

"Mick?" Danny's voice cut through.

"Sorry," Mickey muttered, shaking himself back. "Just… remembering."

"Come on in before we freeze you out there."

* * *

Inside, warmth wrapped around him. Framed pictures lined the walls. A woman's touch was everywhere—Maria's spirit lived in these small things, even if she'd never set foot in this house. Mickey felt her in the hum of the heater, in the glow of the lamps, in the silence that didn't feel empty.

Caleb hovered, still staring at him like a myth stepped off the page.

"You really were champion?" Caleb asked.

"Yup," Mickey said, easing off his cap. "For a little while."

"Did you knock people out?"

Mickey grinned. "Some of 'em. Some knocked me down too. That's the fight game. You win some, you lose some."

Caleb laughed—pure, unguarded. It was Maria's laugh, stitched into Danny's. The sound hit Mickey harder than any punch he'd ever taken, but this time it didn't hurt. It reminded him he was still alive.

They moved into the living room. Caleb peppered him with questions—about gloves, training, fear. Mickey answered every one, slipping in lessons about courage and learning when to stand your ground. He didn't say it outright, but every word was for Danny too.

At one point, Mickey caught Danny's eyes across the room. And there it was—the thing he'd chased his whole life. Pride. Quiet, simple, but real.

Lunch was simple—sandwiches, chips, coffee—but Mickey hadn't felt that full in years. Between bites, he found himself telling stories. Not just of knockouts, but nights after fights—Maria asleep on the couch, Danny curled against him with the belt across their laps, the hum of the TV filling the silence. He hadn't spoken those words in decades, but here, they came like breath.

When Mickey finally stood at the door again, Caleb darted forward and wrapped his arms tight around his waist. Mickey froze, then folded the boy into his arms. For a moment, he let himself believe time had stopped.

"You'll come back, right?" Caleb asked.

"You couldn't keep me away, kiddo," Mickey said with a smile.

Danny clapped his father's shoulder. His voice was steady, but his eyes gave him away. "See you Wednesday?"

"Yeah," Mickey said. The word landed heavy, like a promise, like a bell ringing to end a round.

* * *

Back in his car, Mickey sat still for a long moment. The street was quiet. His chest ached, but lighter now, like he'd dropped a weight he'd been carrying for years.

His eyes drifted to the mirror. Hanging there, frayed and worn, was the rabbit foot. His father's once, then his. For years he'd cursed it, called it a bad-luck charm that carried the Brannigan curse.

He reached up, fingers brushing the stiff fur. For the first time, another thought surfaced: *Maybe it was lucky after all.*

Lucky that he got to stand in his son's doorway. Lucky that he'd been called "Grandfather." Lucky that Maria's voice still lingered in this world, even if only through laughter and memory.

Mickey drove into the fading light with the faintest calm in his chest.

Because the last round wasn't about the crowd or the belt. It was about what you left standing when the bell rang for the final time.

And for once, Mickey Brannigan had left something that mattered. He finished what he started. He truly did save the best for last.

www.ingramcontent.com/pod-product-compliance
Lightning Source LLC
Chambersburg PA
CBHW011325310726
48973CB00011B/3060